100 Reasons to Celebrate

We invite you to join us in celebrating Mills & Boon's centenary. Gerald Mills and Charles Boon founded Mills & Boon Limited in 1908 and opened offices in London's Covent Garden. Since then, Mills & Boon has become a hallmark for romantic fiction, recognised around the world.

We're proud of our 100 years of publishing excellence, which wouldn't have been achieved without the loyalty and enthusiasm of our authors and readers.

Thank you!

Each month throughout the year there will be something new and exciting to mark the centenary, so watch for your favourite authors, captivating new stories, special limited edition collections...and more!

Dear Reader

When anything—a dream, an endeavour, a creation or a relationship—endures, it becomes a legend, an inspiration, a monument, a tale retold the world over. In our hectic times of ephemeral success, anything that endures for years, let alone decades, has become marvelled at and celebrated. But what about something that endures a century—not only any century, but the capricious twentieth century—and grows stronger into the twenty-first? Mills & Boon® and the brand of romance it offers has achieved exactly that—a testimony to its undying appeal and to the vision and talent of all the people who produce the books and comprise the business. It is a great pleasure and pride to be part of something so enduring—something that is at once a dream, an endeavour, a creation and a relationship.

But for me it goes beyond that. Mills & Boon romance novels inspired me, in my life and in my writing, always to search for and to build enduring relationships. In this book I have tried to capture in Malek and Jay all that has ever inspired me in those memorable romances—everything that makes people worthy of an enduring happy-ever-after. I hope you will feel the same way, and I thank you, the discerning reader, for making it all possible.

Happy reading

Olivia Gates

THE SHEIKH SURGEON'S PROPOSAL

BY

OLIVIA GATES

MILLS & BOON®
Pure reading pleasure

First published in Great Britain 2007
Harlequin Mills & Boon Limited,
Eton House, 18-24 Paradise Road, Richmond, Surrey TW9 1SR

ISBN: 978 0 263 86307 9

Set in Times Roman 10 on 12 pt
03-0208-56336

Printed and bound in Spain
by Litografia Rosés, S.A., Barcelona

Olivia Gates has followed many dreams in her life. But there has been only one she was able to pursue single-mindedly, even though it seemed the most impossible of them all: to write romance novels. The fairytale realisation of her dreams came—after years of constantly learning, writing and submitting her manuscripts—when Harlequin Mills & Boon bought her first Medical™ Romance. It was a dream come true, combining her passion—writing—with her vocation—medicine—in one magnificent whole. Now, living with her husband and daughter and their cat, she knows dreams are impish little things. They let you catch them only if you pursue them long and hard enough... Please visit Olivia at her website: http://www.oliviagates.com

Recent titles by the same author:

THE SURGEON'S RUNAWAY BRIDE
THE HEROIC SURGEON
THE DOCTOR'S LATIN LOVER
AIRBORNE EMERGENCY

To my editor, Sheila Hodgson,
for all the guidance that made this book what it is
and made writing it such a pleasure.

To my daughter—
thanks for all the 'naming characters' help.

CHAPTER ONE

JAY LATIMER EXHALED in frustration for the hundredth odd time in the last hour. She muttered something incoherent even to herself, leaned her head on her taxi's window and forced her gaze to take in the vista zooming by, the slice of heaven on earth that was the sprawling pavements and central divider of the most spectacular highway she'd seen in Damhoor so far.

It didn't work. Not even the breathtaking sights of man-engineered beauty of parades of lush palms, immaculate lawns and explosions of flowers and the nature-endowed magic of azure skies and golden sand-seas meeting at the horizon could ameliorate her irritation at having to succumb to this abuse of power.

Just what the hell did Damhoor's Ministry of the Interior think they were doing, *ordering* her to this interview? Making it sound as if they were profiling a foreigner of questionable nature and intentions? Why didn't they just check her credentials and history and be done with it? If half the things she'd heard about their limitless reach and power were true, they probably had dossiers on her from the first moment she'd wailed her indignation at coming into this life. They were reputed to have those on everyone who set foot on their land. So why inconvenience as well as insult her by decreeing this interview?

And that was exactly what they'd done. Decree it. She'd received an honest to goodness summons, at six am no less, specifying the time of said interview only two hours later, and on the far side of Halwan, Damhoor's capital, when they must know it would take her at least two hours to get there. They didn't deem her worthy of even an offer of transportation.

All that when she was here *volunteering* her services.

She hadn't dreamed anything like this would happen when her application two days ago to Global Aid Organization to join the mission that would tour Damhoor's fringe communities and impoverished neighbors had been approved in two minutes flat. She *was* GAO's dream aid worker after all, packing years of emergency medicine experience and promising them open-ended dedication.

Then in had stepped the Ministry of the Interior, over GAO's officials, decreeing it was they who'd decide if volunteers to the mission Damhoor was subsidizing were up to standard, conveniently forgetting that they'd begged for GAO's presence in their region, counting on their experience and logistical clout in humanitarian services to achieve what the kingdom's endless money and resources hadn't been able to.

And here she was, scampering to have some pampered sheikh interrogate her as if she were a suspicious character, to decide if she, her skills and motivations would pass the test of his oblivious, patronizing, over-privileged-from-birth standards!

She exhaled again, trying to bring her temperature under control.

This would be over in no time, she tried to convince herself. This was just a show. Of bravado. Looking a gift horse in the mouth was their way of showing GAO that they didn't really need such gift... *Argh.*

Her rationalizations only made her angrier. Of all the imperious rubbish.

But what did she expect of a land where every higher official belonged to the extensive royal family?

On every level, it seemed her long-held dream of coming to Damhoor was turning into a huge letdown. She'd had nothing but difficulties and rejection since she'd set foot...

She slammed against the window.

The driver had made a sharp swerve. Her heart zoomed into full panic mode as the car careened sideways then crashed into the high sidewalk, coming to a deafening, bone-jarring halt.

In the stillness that consumed the next seconds, she forced herself to breathe, consulted her body. It transmitted one all-important message. No injuries.

Her next thought was for her driver. Her eyes sought him and her heart surged in dismay. He was unconscious, his face covered in blood. *Oh, God...*

Her shaking hands tore her seat belt off and her door open. It was then she saw it, receding in the distance. The reason for their accident. A convoy of three limousines, tearing along the almost deserted highway. Her driver must have lost control over the car while making way for them...

No time for fury. See to him.

She snatched his door open and examined him with eyes and hands. Her searching fingers located the source of his profuse bleeding, a five-inch gash that ran vertically from his scalp, down his forehead and alongside his nose, which was clearly broken. He must have rammed his head on the steering-wheel.

She snatched off her long-sleeved cotton jacket, rummaged in the back for her handbag, grabbed scissors then cut bandages from the jacket. She stemmed his hemorrhage, considering what to do next. With him unconscious and bleeding retronasally, his airway was in imminent danger. He needed to be intubated and ventilated, ASAP.

She had no idea when a highway patrol would pass, what the number for the emergency services was or where the nearest hospital was. And none of the few drivers at this early hour was even slowing down to offer help, beginning with the bastards who'd driven them off the road. If she wanted help, it seemed she'd have to find it herself.

She improvised a cervical collar out of the rest of her jacket then struggled to transfer the man to the passenger seat, taking every care not to exacerbate any spinal injuries.

With her lungs burning and muscles protesting, she took the wheel, started the engine. *Yes.* It was still working.

She floored the gas pedal. She'd make those unfeeling idiots offer the help they hadn't thought they'd owed.

As she hit a hundred miles an hour, she almost slowed down, fearing she'd cause another, this time fatal accident. Only the man who could be choking to death beside her made her maintain her speed. She was about to catch up with the convoy anyway.

It was only when she started overtaking them and waving frantically that they slowed down. About time!

But it was only the lead and rear car that slowed down while the middle one shot forward. Then the cars that had slowed down encroached on her, forcing her to the side of the road. She came to a full stop, her heart hammering as eight huge men dressed in black suits came pouring from the two cars trapping her taxi.

Before she could move, her door was snatched open and she found guns waved in her face and barked orders crashing down on her. They all mostly consisted of "*En'zeli*". Get down.

Get *down*? As in get down on the ground, like an apprehended criminal, hands above her head? Then she realized. In Arabic you got down from a car, not out of it. She guessed that Arabic couldn't always be literally translated into English.

This was one of the hurdles she'd had to leap over before she'd made headway in learning it. The biggest hurdle remained the huge difference between the formal and colloquial forms, the latter being the one being barked in her face right now.

She stepped out of the car, her anger bubbling over.

"Had fun waving your guns at an unarmed woman and an unconscious man?" she snarled. "Now, I demand that you get back in your cars and lead the way to the nearest hospital. And before you do, I need your first-aid kits. I'm sure limos like yours have comprehensive ones!"

Eight pairs of astonished dark eyes stared at her, then at each other. She saw the imperceptible nods they exchanged, then two of them advanced on her and subjected her to a thorough frisking, to her spluttering chagrin.

When they were satisfied she wasn't carrying anything untoward, the one who looked like the leader murmured something into his walkie-talkie. The middle car, which had stopped two hundred feet away, reversed. The guy with the walkie-talkie rushed towards it, and with a great show of deference he opened the passenger door and bowed down to confer with whomever was inside. He straightened with another deep bow and rushed back to her.

"*Ta'ee ma'ee,*" he ordered.

This she also understood. *Come with me.*

"I'm going nowhere with you, and I again demand—"

The man latched onto her arm, cutting her tirade short. She knew her own resistance would make his grip inflict bruises, yet she still struggled and sputtered her indignation all the way to the car. He opened the passenger door, tried to manhandle her in. She snatched herself away, only managing to plop in an unceremonious heap inside. Into what felt like another dimension.

The transition from Damhoor's glaring morning sun into what felt like one of its moonless nights blinded her. And after the intense heat, landing on cool leather had a jolt of goose-bumps storming over her skin. The next thing she noticed was that scent. Pervasive, potent. Pleasurable… It was on account of all those stimuli assaulting her senses that she shook. She was too outraged for alarm to register just yet.

Still blind, she snarled her displeasure. "Is this how you feel like men around here? By ganging up on women after you drive them off the road? But if you think you can get away with anything, I'm telling you I'm—"

Her tirade came to a choking halt. For there they were, materializing out of the blindness. A foot away from her. Eyes, the color of gold and the translucency of pure honey.

They captured hers, forbade her to see or sense anything else, even the person they belonged to. It was only when they finally released her in a sweep of thick black lashes to pour confusion over her that she was freed to take in everything about this man in one unmanageable gulp.

In her haste, she got glimpses of hair the deep gloss of a raven's wing and the relaxed waves of a tranquil sea, skin of polished bronze, slashes and planes and hollows that were all assembled in a composition of—of… Wow.

If she'd ever had any concept of beauty, it had been before she'd seen this—this…man?

Was he a man? Or a being right out of fable?

This would explain that face—a face befitting a higher being. And so was that body. Even an obscuring black suit and shirt did nothing to disguise the daunting breadth and hardness of chest and shoulders, the spareness of waist and hips, the virile power of thighs and the endlessness of legs. Then came that presence that could bend the masses to his merest whim…

And she was being ridiculously fanciful here!

That was, she thought so until her eyes were dragged back to his and she knew they'd been commanded to.

His gaze was even more hard-hitting the second time around, with what she now realized was sleepiness, which he seemed to be having trouble shedding. The sight of the contradictory vulnerability intensified his effect by a factor of a thousand.

But it was the wonder in those eyes that enervated her. The explicit confession that her sight was having an equal impact on him. That the jolt of attraction was mutual.

"Ya Ullah—aish entee?"

His groan reverberated in her bones. *God, what are you?*

And, oh, why wasn't his voice the one thing to shatter the perfection? Like it usually did with beautiful men? It, and what he did with it, was by far his most potent asset. And that was saying way too much.

But what it did shatter was the surreal feeling of being with him in a bubble where time and the rest of the world didn't exist. And her fury rose as if it had never abated.

"What I am," she seethed, "is a very annoyed guest in your country, sir, and I demand that you live up to the legendary chivalry that you advertise as your most prominent quality. The man you drove off the road is suffocating on his blood back in that taxi while you keep me here playing the power games you Damhoorian men seem to revel in!"

Every word lashing out of her mouth wiped the bemusement from his expression, shook off his disorientation. Suddenly clear eyes released hers and he turned away, opened the door and leapt out of the car.

She jumped out of the car right after him. And his men detained her. Frustration exploded out of her in another tirade.

"Sayebooha!" The lash of the man's imperious order made them let her go at once. She hurried after him, found him already examining her unconscious driver.

She leaned over him. "Now you've seen how gravely injured this man is, if you'll please provide me with your first-aid kit..."

His only response was a fierce look over her head, a terse command she didn't get which seemed to magically produce a suitcase-sized emergency bag. Then he took her elbow and moved her away as more abrupt words had his men converging. She understood he'd ordered them to get the driver out of the car.

"No! He has a possible neck injury. You can't move him—not before I stabilize his cervical spine..."

Her frantic words died. The man had opened the bag and was producing a semi-rigid cervical collar. Before she made a grab for it, he turned to her slumped driver, removed her improvised collar and in seconds, and with perfect technique, had his fitted around the man's neck. Then under his continuous orders, his men got the driver out. Specialized EMS personnel wouldn't have done a better job. There was no doubt it was their boss's guidance that made them achieve this result.

Just who *was* this man?

But no matter who he was, or that he seemed versed in the basics of managing a car accident casualty, he couldn't be as experienced as her. She had to take over.

She stood back until the men, still following the constant flow of their boss's precise orders, spread blankets on the hood of one of their limos and placed their casualty there. He had them maneuver the other limo to make its hood a surface for the emergency bag then came to stand at the driver's head.

She rushed to his side then. "Sir, I appreciate your desire to help this man, but if you'll just let me take it from here? I'm a doctor…"

Those eyes, now blazing amber in the sun came up to hers.

"So am I. You're welcome to assist me."

So he was a doctor. That figured. And he spoke perfect English. With a deeply cultured, highly educated British accent to boot. Shouldn't be a surprise. Most well-to-do Damhoorians were educated in the best institutions in the world and England, with its deep ties in the region from its colonial days, was a favorite destination for them. It was still startling to hear that flawless, fathomless drawl flowing out of those spectacular lips. As startling as finding out he was a doctor.

He produced the parts of a hand-held suction machine and expertly snapped them together. She made use of his move, extended her driver's neck gently backwards and performed a jaw thrust. It was the best technique to provide airway patency with the suspicion of neck injury, and the best position to suction his throat. Those amber eyes acknowledged her actions with a glance of approval then resumed his position at the driver's head, inserted the disposable catheter into his throat and turned the machine on.

As soon as blood and secretions shot up into the attached cylinder, her eyes snapped to the bag. Everything was labeled in

Arabic and she wasn't that far into her learning process that she could actually read what the labels said.

As if reading her mind, the man murmured, "The blue bag is the airway kit."

For answer, she swooped down on the indicated bag. In under a minute she had the laryngoscope assembled, the cuffed endotracheal tube, the 10-ml syringe and introducer all ready.

He finished aspirating the driver's throat, took in her measures with another marrow-melting glance of appreciation.

"We won't need rapid sequence anesthesia," he said in that confidential tone colleagues in resuscitation shared. "His gag reflex is absent. We can go ahead with intubation."

She nodded and tossed him a pair of gloves, falling into the synergy of sharing the responsibility for another human being's life with someone who possessed resuscitation experience as extensive as hers. He caught the gloves without batting an eyelid and snapped them on before she'd managed to snap hers on.

Then it started.

And it was as if they'd been managing critical patients in the field together for years, collaborating with the merest of looks and partial murmurs, delineating their needs and obtaining the other's support. In under two minutes they had an endotracheal tube inserted and connected to a self-expanding bag-valve-mask and their patient ventilated with 100 percent oxygen.

Then they turned to handling circulation.

She measured blood pressure as he took the man's pulse. Then they exchanged findings.

He exhaled. "Not good. He's going into shock."

She only nodded, reached for two 18-gauge over-the-needle catheters. "I'll go for bilateral IV access for quickest fluid replacement."

In answer, he applied tourniquets, prepared two bags of Ringer's as she slipped one catheter after another into the driver's cephalic veins, each on the first try. She withdrew the needles and he snapped off the tourniquets, attached the tubing to the giving sets and set the drips to maximum.

His eyes moved from watching the uninterrupted flow of fluid into the driver's veins, stilled on her. Then he finally shook his head, as if to clear it. "All right. That's A, B and C. On to D."

His murmur snapped her out of the fugue state she seemed to fall into each time his eyes fell on her.

She scrambled to join in assessing the driver's neurological status using the Glasgow coma score.

With a GCS of fifteen as fully conscious and three as deeply comatose, the driver's nine wasn't good, but it still boded well for no irreversible neurological damage. E—or exposure—revealed no other gross injuries. So they turned to the patient's major one. He cut off her improvised, and now soaked and leaking, pressure bandage and the scalp wound spurted again. She jumped in with another bandage.

He sighed. "You didn't sacrifice your jacket for nothing. At this rate, he would have gone into shock in minutes without your pressure bandage. This uncontrollable bleeding indicates a serious bleeding-clotting disorder."

She thought so too. Even with the scalp being one of the areas best supplied with blood vessels in the body, leading to alarming and not easily controlled bleeding, this was in a different league from any scalp injury she'd ever handled.

"What I'd give for cautery right now," she said.

He simply unzipped another bag and produced a cautery probe.

Her mouth fell open. "What else do you have in there? A full OR?"

His lips twitched as he turned on the machine and handed it to her. She jumped on the offending bleeders, zapped them closed as he blotted blood for her. When she'd gotten them all, she turned it off and cleaned it as he applied meticulous pressure once more, concluding their resuscitation efforts.

The man exhaled, stretching up to what she now realized was

a truly daunting height. He was about a foot taller than her five feet six. "He's stable for now," he said. "And once he has the benefit of definitive investigations and management, I think he'll be as good as new in a few days."

She believed so too. Thanks to his intervention and preparedness. *If* no thanks to his carelessness and recklessness that had caused the accident in the first place. The reminder brought her outrage bubbling to the surface once more.

"It's all well and good that you helped stabilize him. *Now* will you make one of your cars lead the way to the nearest hospital, where this man can get definitive management?"

He blinked, her renewed resentment clearly taking him by surprise. Then he only extended his hand to her.

With no conscious decision to do so, she gave him the hand he'd demanded. He barely held it as he escorted her back to his car, seated her with every care and courtesy then walked around the car and sat down beside her.

She stared at him, wondering what had just happened, feeling her hand sizzling from that contact with his.

He got out his cellphone, dialed one number after another and let rip in Arabic. This time she didn't get one word of the deeply colloquial torrent.

Just a second before she exploded, he terminated his last call and turned to her, his lips spreading, his teeth a stunning flash.

Everything inside her jangled with that blast of charisma. This man shouldn't be allowed to smile in inhabited areas.

"Everything has been taken care of," he said.

Really? Just like that, huh?

And she let him have it. "So your reckless driving causes someone's near-death and you just make a few phone calls and you wipe the record clean, huh? How wonderful it must be to possess enough power to walk all over people, rewrite history and come up smelling like roses!"

His bone-liquefying smile teetered. But just for seconds. Then it was widening, his incredible eyes narrowing, heating up. It enraged her more, made her even more fluent in her abuse.

"So how have you reconstructed the accident?" she plowed on. "That you stopped of your own accord and rushed to help the poor driver? What have you decided made him crash? Speeding under the influence of alcohol or…?"

He placed one finger over her lips. And she went mute.

The feel of the smooth, tough skin on hers, the masculinity and power and that scent that was all him inundating her, almost making her pass out with the pressure of sensations… Too much!

Just get out of here. Get away from him.

"Look, as long as you take care of my driver, I guess you can do whatever you please—as I'm sure you will anyway. So I'll just go now." She cursed herself for the wobble in her voice. "You've already made me an hour late for my appointment."

All lightness seeped from his gaze, something single-minded flaring there. "You don't need to worry about that. About anything." Then he lowered the barrier between them and his driver and ordered, "*Seeda.*"

The powerful car shot forward instantly, soundlessly, eating up the asphalt, taking her who knew where.

A minute later she finally found her voice. "Can you, please, order your driver to stop? I'll take another taxi."

"Do you see an abundance of taxis around here?"

"That's my problem."

"I beg to differ."

"Listen, I have the number of the company that sent me the first taxi. I'll call them. So thanks for the thought, but if you just let me get down here, I'll get out of your hair and—"

"Now, that's a lovely image—you in my hair." He looked sideways at her as he sprawled beside her like a lion settling down to a nap. "Why would I want you out of it?"

"You're not letting me go?"

He just smiled. And she cried, "Are you kidnapping me?"

He laughed. A sound of such beauty and impact it was cruel. "Now there's an idea. And who would blame me? When a dream pursues a man, he lets himself get caught, captures her back."

A dream? So he'd progressed from toying with her to mocking her!

"I—I didn't pursue you," she muttered. "I just had to make you stop and take responsibility for your callous behavior."

"What callous behavior? I wasn't driving. And my drivers swear they didn't notice the accident they had caused." Before she flayed him with more sarcasm, he talked across her intended rebuke. "But I *do* assume responsibility for their haste. I was rushing to an appointment, told them of my wish to conclude it in record time so I'd finally get to bed. It seems they were blind to anything but fulfilling my wishes."

Though he had shown such care to the injured driver, his explanations left a lot to be desired. She opened her mouth to flay him again and he went on talking, obliterating the last of her irritation, vaporizing any retorts and thoughts.

"I don't consider this an apology," he murmured. "Or that one is enough to make up for the accident I indirectly caused and which I can only thank God wasn't any worse and that you weren't injured. Your driver is being airlifted to the best hospital in Halwan, he will get comprehensive treatment, follow-up and compensation, and his car will be replaced. As for my failure to intervene, you must excuse me. I was sleeping until my head guard woke me up, saying that a foreign woman had intercepted us and they believed she was mad, if not armed." He huffed a laugh, all dismissal and irony. "Which shows how clueless they are." His gaze swept her in one hot, total body caress that singed her down to the bone. "You are more than armed. You are lethal."

Her nerves fired an all-out alarm. Her heart was racing itself to a standstill.

What was happening to her? She'd never reacted to a man, to

anything, like that. That runaway reaction, suffocating in intensity, transporting in headiness.

Feeling so out of her depth made her angrier.

"And you are...forward," she choked. "But what do I expect from a man who's rushing to bed—now? In the aftermath of a night of excess, no doubt."

He took her jeering with another enervating smile, the smile of a man who was certain he'd never be less than the ultimate in any woman's eyes.

Then he finally spoke, deep and devastating. "I hope by the time I take you to your appointment you'll think more kindly of me. Now, if you'll excuse me." He flipped open his cellphone. "I'll just arrange a postponement of mine."

He took his eyes off her only long enough to punch in a number. And at that exact moment her phone rang.

She fumbled it out, groaning inwardly. That Ministry of Interior hotshot must be fuming by now. She wondered if he'd believe she'd had an accident or if he'd think she was just incapable of being punctual. It was all she needed, starting off on the wrong foot with the man who could send her packing!

She punched the answer button, croaked a wavering "Hello?"

An endless moment of silence met her tentative greeting.

Then she finally heard an answering, "Hello."

The problem was, she heard that same hello in stereo.

Out of her cellphone, and out of her companion's lips.

CHAPTER TWO

MALEK HEARD THE melodic "hello" pouring into his ear from his phone and simultaneously washing over him from his companion's full, flushed lips.

He stared at her, shared a suspended moment of incomprehension.

Then he burst out in guffaws.

She was the doctor he'd been rushing to meet.

This was unbelievable. He couldn't have dreamed anything like this would happen when he'd taken over the chore of approving the latest addition to GAO's personnel in Damhoor.

He only had because he didn't trust Shaaker from Interior to perform the interview with the necessary finesse. He also had to meet this doctor, make sure he—or, as it turned out, she—understood what working in the region entailed. Most people came there thinking that working in Damhoor, one of the richest kingdoms in the world, would be a luxury, and those false expectations had caused many setbacks. He wanted to stem potential trouble in advance.

Since he hadn't known when he could slot this interview into his hectic schedule, he'd decided to do it the second he had a couple of hours of freedom. This would have left him around three hours to sleep before his next chore, but after weeks of fractions of an hour of exhausting oblivion, three hours still felt like a luxury.

On his way to this interview, he'd drifted into another fitful episode of unconsciousness the moment he'd hit his seat and had jolted awake to this—this vision.

There was no other word to describe her. And that's when his tastes had always gravitated towards dark beauty. Or so he'd thought until he'd seen this incandescent creature.

There was no doubt what his preference was now, or would remain. It had formed the moment he'd seen her. It was now hair with every gradation of the colors of the dunes of his kingdom, eyes that reflected the azure of its skies and the translucence of its seas, complexion of its richest cream and rarest honey and features and a body caressed into being by God. It was *her.*

He'd never known such attraction, so much so he'd at first wondered if his exhausted mind had been playing tricks on him. But not any more. Not after that incredible experience of tending her injured driver with her, and everything that had come before and after it. Every word lashing him, every glance penetrating him, every breath singeing him. It was real. More than real. It was overwhelming him into breaking a code he'd lived by since he'd turned seventeen. A code he'd thought unbreakable.

He never made the first move towards a woman. Or the second, or the last. It had been he who had received advances, and had shunned them mostly. That had still left many, maybe even too many he'd decided to accept. But he had a take-it-or-leave-it attitude, always making sure these women were totally free to make such advances, were looking for similar transient entertainment and understood in advance the details of what to expect from him. Utmost courtesy, thorough gratification—and whatever he saw fit to bestow on them besides that—and an amicable, swift and final parting of the ways.

But none of that applied here. His code, his rules were nowhere to be found. And that when she'd certainly made no advances, in any form, just the opposite. While he was certainly making them. And though indignant, and resistant, she, too, was at the mercy of this incredible affinity. He was certain of it.

He now held those eyes that had so far reflected such an entrancing mixture of steel and softness, resourcefulness and guilelessness. They were now twin displays of total shock.

Then he spoke into his phone. "And here I thought the Jay Latimer I was on my way to meet was a man. This has to be the misunderstanding of a lifetime."

And he was now certain why Shaaker had tried his best to dissuade him from taking over this meeting. The sly desert jackal hadn't wanted to give the opportunity up.

Malek chuckled at how things had turned out, at the way she kept the phone glued to her ear, her stare widening.

"I guess I don't need to tell you what kept me from our appointment," he murmured again, still into the phone. "Or beg your forgiveness for having to be even later."

She snatched her phone from her ear as if it had burned her, looked from it and back to him in what he could only describe as horror. And he couldn't believe how her distress disturbed him.

He snapped his phone shut and turned fully to her, anxious to dispel it, and the change in his position brought his thigh against hers, only managing to deepen her—and his—agitation.

He readjusted his pose, severed the contact. Even when it was the last thing he wanted to do. He just had to soothe her.

"If not for the accident," he began, keeping his voice tranquil, as if gentling a skittish mare, "and for my and my men's role in it, I'd say this is a very happy occasion. For us to meet before the arranged time, over a matter of life and death… There's no introduction to beat coming together to fight for another's life. You must agree this just has to be fate."

And Jay agreed. A cruel one.

He was the one who'd evaluate her eligibility? That big shot from Damhoor's Ministry of Interior or rather, with him being a doctor, from the Ministry of Health?

And she'd insulted him in every way she could think of!

That was, she had between the episodes when she'd stared at him open-mouthed and glassy-eyed betraying her helpless reaction to him. Still, she was sure he was used to such a reaction. He no doubt waded in women who threw themselves at his feet and pursued him to any lengths. And while she'd never do either, just that he must have read her reactions made this situation untenable.

Even if he hadn't noticed her almost swooning, just sitting near him, he'd noticed her heaping disdain on him without pausing to ask who he was. Not the level-headed professional image she'd hoped to project…

"So is Jay your real name, or is it an initial?" His question severed her hectic contemplations, the intimacy permeating his awesome voice fizzing in her blood.

It took seconds to process his question, to force herself out of her trance to choke an answer. "It's—it's an initial."

"Standing for…?" he pressed moments later when she didn't elaborate.

"Janaan," she croaked.

"Janaan?" His hushed tone attested to his astonishment far more than a shout would have. A long moment passed when only the smooth whir of the engine permeated the silence, then he inclined his head at her, his eyes probing, tinged with wonder. "That's an Arabic name."

Oh, yes, she knew that. All too well.

"And not any Arabic name. But *Janaan*." He said her name as if he were tasting it, made it sound lush and unique, almost magical, a name she'd always been uncomfortable with, had never used in full. "Will your surprises never cease?"

He waited, as if he expected her to answer. When she just stared back at him mutely, he exhaled, sat forward, extended his hand to her. And this time, when she once more gave him hers without volition, his grip was neither feathery nor ephemeral.

"Well, Janaan Latimer of the ceaseless surprises, we've met

under difficult circumstances. Let's start again, shall we?" He gave her hand a tiny squeeze. "It was a great honor to work with you, and as great a pleasure to make your acquaintance. I am Dr. Malek Aal Hamdaan, at your service."

Every word he uttered was like an electric current jolting through her heart. She felt she was suffocating on it as she groped for something to say, something to stop his advance through her barriers. "I prefer Jay—or—or Dr. Latimer…"

He waved this hand of his, the epitome of strength and elegance, the very expression of power and entitlement. "You'll have to forgive me for defying your wishes, but now I know your name, I can never call you anything but Janaan."

She opened her mouth to contest his presumption, to insist on keeping the distance of formality—and realization knocked her mouth shut on the semi-formed protest.

He was an Aal Hamdaan. That was the name of the royal family of Damhoor. He was one of them!

Of course he was, moron.

Hadn't she known she was on her way to meet some sheikh who had his position by having been born a royal? And though she'd had a ridiculously inaccurate mental image of him, that Malek was that sheikh should have been the first thing she'd realized the moment she'd heard his voice mocking her on the other end of the line.

But that was assuming she had any mental faculties left functional. She was sinking deeper into shock. And it only made her angrier that even now his effect on her was deepening.

"I may not be able to stop you from calling me whatever you want," she quavered. "But don't blame anyone but yourself if I refuse to answer to anything but the names I specified."

He went totally still. He didn't even give off any vibes. She couldn't tell what his reaction to her impertinence was. Or maybe that stillness was answer enough.

Then he moved closer, and drawled, "Can you be this cruel?

Depriving me of the pleasure of calling you by this name that so suits you?"

"Since it's a stupid name, I now know what you think of me." But he'd be right. She *was* being stupid. Big time.

She'd always held her tongue, never voiced her ready, blunt opinions. But now, when she should be exercising her lifelong restraint most, here she was doing her best to offend and alienate this man who must have oodles of power, who was the one who had the say in whether she'd stay in Damhoor. Where she so desperately wanted to stay.

But contrary to looking offended and alienated, he seemed elated. "How can you even think that a name that means one's very heart and mind and soul is stupid? And beyond its evocative meaning, its very sound is exquisite—refined, flowing, feminine. Surely you know you more than live up to it, in every way?"

Did this guy have an advanced degree in flirtation? If there were some championship in it, he must hold the title. But *was* he flirting? It felt as if he meant every word.

Of course you'd like to think that, idiot.

And then what would she do with his sincere admiration? He was so out of her league and this was so transient that even letting herself feel good about it—if she could feel anything in her agitation, that was—was pointless.

Then he added to her agitation. "So, Janaan Latimer, now our appointment has become irrelevant, I can think of nothing better than to escort you to an early lunch."

Jay gaped. This—this god was asking her out to lunch?

OK, so he was *telling* her he was taking her to lunch, but it amounted to the same thing. And she was certain he hadn't intended to take the man he'd thought he'd meet out to lunch.

So was it because the unusual circumstances had broken the formality with which he would have received her had things gone to plan? Or was it that he wanted to prolong their time together as his eyes were telling her, as his words corroborated?

And just what was it with her today?

He was just being courteous, and she was constructing intricate delusions on what she thought she saw in his eyes, heard in his words. She'd been having what she could only call a breakdown of sanity since she'd laid eyes on him!

She shook her head to dispel the feeling of sinking deeper under a spell, his spell. "Thanks for the generous offer, but I have to decline. And I don't see why our appointment has become irrelevant. We can still have the interview. We can even have it here. If you'll just ask me what you intended to, then let me take a taxi back to my hotel, I'd be most grateful."

Malek stared at Janaan as if she'd started talking in a language he'd never heard before.

She'd just refused him.

He'd invited her to lunch and she'd *refused* him.

So he hadn't exactly invited her, he amended inwardly. He'd stated his desire to have her company, his intention to have it, not for a second thinking there was any possibility of her turning him down.

But she had. Not only that, but she'd done it with such an adorable mixture of resoluteness, hauteur and shyness that it was all he could do to stop himself from reaching out and hauling her into his arms. Which would be crazy.

But with every passing second it seemed less crazy, was becoming all he could think of doing… *Ehda ya rejjal.*

His self-rebuke to calm down wasn't all that brought the overpowering urge under precarious control. Just the thought that he might distress her in any way—though he was certain she hadn't feared him for a second—was enough to leash him in.

He still couldn't stop himself from leaning closer into her aura, watching her, greedy for her every nuance as he murmured, "We've already discussed the impossibility of me leaving you here, or anywhere else. And we can conduct our interview all that much better over a meal cooked with passion and to perfection and served with all the charm and cordiality of my kingdom. As you've already pointed out, you're a guest in my land. Let me show you how valued you are, let me give you a welcome worthy of you."

He marveled at her reaction, at its explicitness. He could feel his every word's impact on her, could sense her reeling, struggling to right herself. He was certain she was fighting the urge to blurt out an acceptance, was convinced she'd delivered her first refusal as an involuntary conditioning not to accept a man's overtures at once. Yet from her reaction it was clear she hadn't thought he'd press her, was flailing now that he had.

He was incapable of doing anything else. He had to have more of her. She had to accept. And any moment now, she would.

She inhaled a deep breath. He did, too, held it, waiting for the words that would assure him of more time with her.

"That's very generous of you," she started, a delightful wobble making a heart-tingling tremolo of every second syllable. *Yes.* Her next words would be the craved acceptance. "But I again insist on concluding this now." *What?* "I am a guest in Damhoor only in terms of being new here, but I'm not here as a tourist. I'm here to work. So if we can just get down to business, this would be the only welcome I'd appreciate."

Anticipation whooshed out of him, frustration rushing in to fill its void, shooting to unknown levels.

No one had ever refused him before. Not once, let alone twice. Certainly never a woman. It was he who refused women's offers, had never been interested enough to make any himself.

Now he was, and he'd offered, twice, and twice she'd turned him down.

It had to be his offering skills. They were non-existent. He'd better develop some. Fast.

But until he got his bearings, found out how she could be approached, her reticence overcome, he needed time and… Wait!

She *had* just given him the key to securing that time, far longer than what the most leisurely lunch could have afforded him.

He smiled down on her. "So you're interested in getting down to business, eh? How about we bypass the interview and head directly to where business is conducted? Surely you wouldn't refuse me escorting you to your new base on Damhoorian soil."

She blinked. "What…? Where do you mean?"

"GAO's newly opened base of operations in the kingdom. As I understand it, you signed up in the old office. I think you'll be very interested to see the new facilities and go over the specifics of GAO's expanded mission in the region."

She stared at him, a dozen emotions struggling for dominance over her expressive features. Chagrin, interest, frustration, curiosity, agitation, bashfulness. He was interested in one in particular right now. Capitulation.

When he judged it had overridden all other reactions, he whispered his challenge, "So what will it be, Janaan?"

She gulped, another rush of peach staining her velvet cheeks. Then she finally sighed. "Oh, all right."

Her muttered concession was the most welcome thing he'd ever heard in his life. It was also the last thing she said. At least the longest. He only managed to get monosyllables out of her from then on. He was certain it was her way of showing him how angry she was that he'd cornered her, that she'd succumbed to his maneuvers. He was also certain anger was a mere impurity tainting her real emotions, all hot and eager and overriding.

He got to her as badly as she got to him. And the best and unprecedented thing was that it was him who got to her, not who he was.

He knew she had no idea who he was as she was treating him with no deference at all. Even after she'd found out he was someone important, at least to her, she'd remained as painfully, delightfully forthright as she'd been from moment one. He doubted she'd change her tune even when she found out exactly who he was. This was another unprecedented occurrence that he…

"Is this it?"

Her subdued yet awed question brought him out of his elated musings.

And, indeed, their destination was in sight. The sprawling establishment erected to serve the joint efforts of GAO and his kingdom's Ministry of Health.

Its sight somehow brought reality and full wakefulness descending on him with a flat-fisted thump.

What in Ullah's name had he been thinking, feeling—doing?

What did he think he was about to do?

He should drop her off, give orders for her to be given every courtesy and service as long as she stayed in Damhoor and make sure he never saw her again.

CHAPTER THREE

"IS SOMETHING WRONG?"

Malek saw Janaan's clear blue eyes clouding with confusion, and wondered how to answer her.

"*Everything* is wrong" didn't appeal as a reply. Even though it was the only answer. The truth.

If he'd succumbed to this lightning-bolt attraction within minutes of meeting her, and now had to exert all his will to keep his hands off her, who knew what he'd be tempted to do if he had her in close proximity for much longer?

The answer to that was certain. And if he'd thought he had enough upheavals to deal with, those certainly paled in comparison with what any level of involvement with her—a foreign woman and a doctor coming to his region in a worthy relief effort—would be. It was out of the question that he…

"OK, I don't feel the extra head I've grown." Janaan ran both her hands over her head. "But the look in your eyes is making me certain it's there."

And he laughed. *Ya Ullah*, that was all he needed. To find out she had a sense of humor. One that tickled him so readily.

"It would be more of a good thing in your case." He barely caught back the hand that longed to mimic her actions and shook his head, attempting to clear it, to shake off the urge. "I apologize for blanking out on you. It seems I'm not fully awake."

And what he wouldn't give to blame exhaustion for it all. But he couldn't. He'd been exposed to many kinds of danger in his life, but nothing compared to the potential hazard of prolonging his exposure to her. Sanity was crying out for him to end this. And he would. He had to.

He dropped her gaze, stepped out of the car the moment it came to a halt, came around to her.

He thought it a terrible idea to touch her again but out of bounds of his will, his hand asked for hers. "Shall we?"

She gave it to him, her own inability to resist surging with her color, her lips trembling as she sprang out of the car at the same moment he gave her a supporting tug. Both actions brought her full against him.

It was only a second before Janaan staggered back, severing the contact. And that second had been enough to tell him that his worst projections were nothing. His body had never roared with arousal like that.

"S-so…w-when did all this get built?"

He looked down at her and his chest tightened with regret. She glowed under his kingdom's sun, from the inside out. He narrowed his eyes against her radiance more than against the sun, read her attempt to jog him back to reality.

She succeeded in making him aware of their audience. His men, hovering around, waiting for his orders. He turned to them and delivered them. Arranging the end of this magical interlude.

With his plan in motion he felt less guilty, even felt entitled to let his hand run up her exposed arm, wrap around its satin resilience as he steered her inside the building, telling himself that the shudder that engulfed his body was due to the transition from the blistering heat to the interior's coolness.

He would take this with her, say and do what felt natural. It would be over soon. Too soon. He wouldn't let the upcoming separation pollute the time he'd allowed himself with her.

He relaxed his knotted brow, smiled down at her. "In delayed answer to your question, the construction was finished four months ago, the rest two weeks or so ago. We're staffing now."

Jay was barely conscious of the people in the background or those who were lining up like a welcoming committee ahead. She only had eyes for Malek as she hurried to keep up with his far longer strides. What she couldn't keep up with was the dizzying succession of expressions on his face. One second he'd looked elated, the next pensive, then harsh, then upset and now, though he was back to being plain overwhelming, she could feel his…conflict. There was no other way to describe what was coming off him in waves. What was going on inside that mind of his?

As if she'd ever find out. Or should want to. He was probably only regretting his behavior, which he'd explained the reason for. Lack of sleep made people do and say things they didn't mean. Now he'd rush her on a tour because he'd committed himself to it then he'd drop her in GAO's lap and head to his bed at last.

This explanation somehow put her at ease. Confusion agitated her. But knowing the whys and wherefores of all this, that it would be over soon, made her equilibrium, and another form of spontaneity, resurface. She felt she could allow herself the luxury of basking in his presence for as long as it lasted.

She looked up at him, fighting the urge to reach up and brush back the lock of hair that had slipped down his forehead, to run her palm over the darkness roughening the satin of his chiseled cheeks and jaw, and smiled her pleasure at just being near him. "And how are the staffing efforts going?"

Tension and weariness drained from his eyes as his smile widened to match hers. "With you here? Spectacularly."

She giggled. Why not let herself feel good about the incredible things that kept spilling from his spectacular lips?

He chuckled, too, gave her a conspiratorial glance. "Don't look now, but it seems all existing staff have come out in force to welcome you."

Her lips twisted. "Yeah, right. They're standing on attention for their commander-in-chief's surprise inspection. Quaking in their shoes, no doubt."

His mock-hurt look was simply delicious. "You don't think it possible they're just thrilled to see me?"

"You know what? From their smiles, I bet they are." And who wouldn't be? she added inwardly.

"Tell you what…" A gentle tug turned her to face their reception party. "Let's get the introductions out of the way so they get back to their work and we get on with our tour."

For the next fifteen minutes they did just that. Jay counted fourteen different nationalities among the GAO volunteers, in addition to the Damhoorians, in every medical and administrative position, about a hundred in all. But a place that size would need thirty times more personnel to run it. Not that she was sure just what this place was supposed to be.

After a gracious command from Malek made everybody rush to leave them alone, Jay fell into step with him as he took her on a thorough tour of the premises and facilities.

And if she'd been impressed by its sheer size from the outside, she was flabbergasted now. She'd never seen anything this comprehensive. It was far more than a medical complex. The diagnostic and treatment sectors, once staffed, could easily deal with mass casualty situations. Supplies, warehousing, food services and housekeeping could keep up with an army's logistics and supply chain in a year-long war. The teaching and training facilities in all fields could spawn legions of highest caliber medical and administrative professionals. The research sector had all the promise of being at the cutting edge in science and healthcare. The administrative and managerial sectors could probably run a country, and so could the seamless mechanical, electronic and telecommunications systems. This place was a mind-boggling triumph of ambition and efficiency.

It was only confusing that GAO had built it in Damhoor, where the average citizen had an income to rival that of the richest countries in the world and a comprehensive medical insurance.

They were now in the last section, diagnostics, and he gave her another comprehensive summation of its capabilities. Then he spread his formidable arms, stretching his black shirt across his expansive chest, like a magician inviting applause.

Stunned hunger at his power-laden grace was probably what stopped her from clapping. She couldn't believe how entertaining he'd made the technical data he'd inundated her with.

His grin, this amalgam of teasing and enjoyment wrapped up around a core of unadulterated maleness, flashed at her. "I hope I haven't overloaded and crashed your system."

"So this was your plan, huh? To make me sorry for insisting on getting down to business by immersing me in a vat of it."

He pouted. "I'd never want to make you sorry. But you're such an informed listener that I got carried away. The desire to brag was also something I couldn't apply brakes to." He stopped before they reached the exit doors. "But seriously, have I bored you?"

Jay didn't think it wise to inform him he was probably genetically incapable of being boring. That she'd be an avid listener to him reciting the *Yellow Pages*.

Instead she smirked. "As if I'd tell you if you had."

"Oh, you would. I believe that you of all people would whack me over the head with your candid opinion, no matter what."

"Gee—I was that rude earlier, huh?"

"You only said what you thought. And then you were rattled from the accident, you were fighting for your driver's life, and you were maybe a little frightened you'd fallen into some depraved man's clutches."

"Two out of three there, pal." One of his eyebrows went up and her heat shot in the same direction. She was really forgetting who he was. Who she was. *Somebody gag and sedate her.*

"Care to elaborate?" he prompted.

"Uh—just that I wasn't scared of you for a second." His eyes flared at that, with something akin to—pride? Satisfaction? Giving up on trying to interpret his expression, she went on,

"Maybe stupid, but there you go. And listen—about that last crack. I have this social deficiency syndrome and it's complicated by a severe case of verbal communication atrophy…"

"Don't apologize," he admonished. "I loved it. Even if I didn't, you still shouldn't apologize. *Never* apologize, Janaan."

Oh, God—the way he said her name!

"Uh, I'm not apologizing, actually," she mumbled, feeling a strange elasticity in her knees. "Just confessing my condition."

His eyes crinkled. "I hope it's incurable."

"You don't need to hope too hard. It probably is."

His look as he led her out of the building was mystery itself. But it was the lines of tiredness that stamped his heart-stopping beauty that made her heart, and hands, itch, wanting to soothe them away.

She barely noticed they were approaching his convoy. She only felt his gentleness as he once again seated her in his car, in the blessed welcome of cool darkness and his proximity.

He didn't order his driver to drive, only adjusted his position to face her. "So, what do you think of GAO Central?"

"Besides 'holy cow', you mean…?" She stopped, groaned. "That probably isn't the right exclamation to make around here…"

A powerful finger stemmed her mumbling. "What have I told you about never apologizing?" She couldn't hold back the shudder the feel of his finger on her lips, his words, his voice wrenched from her. "Before you tell me you're not, I want you to promise me never to watch what you say around me." Yeah, sure. For the whole of the next hour. She could do that. "I have no cultural or religious sensitivities to step on. Even if I did, I think political correctness is becoming reverse persecution and I for one am never contributing to it. 'Holy cow' summed up your opinion beautifully."

Not only a god, but deeply sane with it too. Whoa.

She cleared her throat, groped for something half-coherent to say. "Not that my opinion counts for much, but this place is awesome—as you know. But what, and why, is it? I didn't know

GAO had anywhere near these resources or, if they did, that they'd use them to establish a single mammoth of a center like this."

He smile was all indulgence. "You're right. GAO wouldn't splurge on one place like that. This is all built by Damhoorian funds, providing GAO with a site to pool resources, human and otherwise, to engineer emergency and long-term operations, to equip, man and deploy them, as well as a destination for those in need of help, medical or otherwise, who GAO can't help with any reliability or continuity under the conditions in their countries."

She chewed her lip. "Put that way, this place is the answer to the prayers of all the people I know who work with GAO. They always moan about how prosperous nations can do far more to help them in their humanitarian endeavors and aren't. But this place says that one of those nations is. And doing it right."

He gave a dismissive gesture. "We haven't done much yet."

"You've done plenty and laid the foundations for doing a lot more. And in such economy. That's one of the things that most impressed me here—the total lack of opulence."

He huffed in what looked like genuine surprise. "Excuse me, but you're the first to comment favorably on that. Everyone took me to task about what was described as the barrenness of the place."

"It's not barren!" she protested. "It has great ambiance and it's streamlined. Guess everyone's been brainwashed by the five-star medical complexes sprouting up all over the world. It makes my blood boil to think of all the people who could have been helped with all the money that went to their zillion-dollar internal decoration. But this place is simple and efficient and its size is purely functional. It's clear every cent was well spent."

His smile widened. "You have issues with misspent money, don't you?"

She frowned. "Any sane human being has those."

"You'd be surprised how many *in*sane human beings litter the planet, then. But GAO's positive influence goes beyond cost-effectiveness. This establishment is as near perfection as it gets in terms of therapeutic environment, sanitation, circulation, expandability, safety, security and sustainability and I've already commissioned them to design a major health center in Al Areesha, our major coastal city."

She nodded slowly. "Um—I'm still not clear why GAO is basing itself here, in one of a handful of countries in the world where its presence isn't needed. Why not take your donations and build many mini-centers in their target regions?"

"Because being here..." He spread those expressive hands of his. "...on Damhoorian soil, gives GAO a stable base of operations and the vast resources to reach out to the chaotic and impoverished countries in the region. Damhoor also has fringe communities that need their awareness raised in order to provide them with effective healthcare, to stop them from abusing their health in the name of tradition. We've learned that wealth and resources have no impact on such deep-rooted problems. So, yes, even Damhoor needs GAO for their unsurpassed experience in dealing with every cultural and mass health dilemma known to man."

Just what she'd been thinking before the accident. Before she'd met him, a lifetime ago. And he was admitting it, so freely, so eloquently. Not at all the attitude she'd expected. But, then, what preconception of hers hadn't he pulverized?

And she was spending the last minutes in his company. Now he'd take her back to her hotel. She doubted she'd ever see him again.

A fist convulsed around her heart. Which was just silly.

But, silly or not, after the soaring of the last hours she felt like she was on a roller-coaster. Meeting him had been one hell of a ride. Now she was on the last drop before she got off.

Just get it over with.

"So, uh, I get the picture now," she croaked. "And it looks great. You were, too—helping me with my driver, taking me around the base, going above and beyond in debriefing me." She rummaged in her bag for her hotel address and handed it to him.

He scowled down at it.

"Is this an attempt at subtlety?" he drawled, slow and nerve-racking. "Demanding I take you to your hotel without actually saying so?"

She gave an awkward shrug. "I must get points for not blurting out the demand like before. And you notice I'm no longer asking to get out to take a taxi."

"Only because you're too intelligent to try the same thing again and expect a different result."

"That doesn't take intelligence, just common sense." She stopped, her heart slamming against her ribs until she felt he must see them throbbing through her top. "I—I hope you'll let one of your men update me about my driver's condition."

"He's our patient. *My* patient." That had an edge of harshness, of arrogance, betraying another side of him. The side no one would want to cross. It seemed he couldn't abide her allusion that he'd relegate the responsibility. "*I'll* follow him up and update you."

Something thorny expanded in her throat. She could only nod, before turning blind eyes to the darkened vista outside her window. Let him ask the driver to get going. Let them get to her hotel quickly. Please.

She felt him move beside her, felt as if every muscle expanding and contracting under his polished bronze skin was pulling at her own. Then his voice drenched her skin in goose-bumps.

"About our interview," he drawled huskily, commanding her eyes back to his, his gaze on her mesmerizing, "and conducting it over the now very late lunch—what cuisine takes your fancy? French, Italian, Chinese—or local?"

CHAPTER FOUR

HE WAS INSANE.

Instead of sticking to his plan of taking Janaan on a short guided tour then rushing her back to one of his cars and jumping in another to zoom in the opposite direction, he'd gone over the base almost down to the wiring and piping, clung to her all the way to his car and jumped in beside her telling himself he couldn't hand her over to his driver and must escort her himself to her hotel. Then she'd let him know exactly where to drop her and he'd panicked. He'd known then that his plans had been empty bravado, that he'd do anything to prolong his time with her.

And he had. He'd taken her to one of his two "personal" places. His first and overwhelming desire had been to take her to his private one. A last wisp of sanity had made him opt for the public one, even if it was where he'd never brought another woman.

He was still vibrating with the jumble of relief and anxiety that had assailed him when she'd succumbed this time, with such an obvious muddle of eagerness and agitation. She felt the same about him, knew it was foolish to prolong the exposure, yet couldn't stop herself either.

But if there'd be no more brakes applied from her side, how high would this conflagration soar?

She now snatched her eyes away, sent a tremulous smile up

at the Bedouin waiter who'd placed the last in over a dozen plates of hors d'oeuvres on the four-foot-round copper tray. Then she busied herself with smoothing the *keleem* covering the floor where she sat, studying the vivid patterns of the hand-woven wool before she tucked her blue denim-covered legs beneath her, adjusting her pose against the reclining cushion into a guarded, formal one. She could have been spreading herself in the most erotic display with the way his hormones seethed.

His avid gaze followed her nervous, awed one as it darted around. She was attempting to distract herself with the details of the restaurant, which was a vision of the time of one thousand and one nights with a futuristic twist.

It was minutes, crowded with the unspoken and the out of bounds, before she finally gave up trying to avoid his eyes and a conversation, and sighed. "So you own this place, or what?"

He huffed in surprise at this new self-deprecation she made him experience. "It's just the only place, besides one of my retreats, where I feel...at peace."

"Provided you're the only customer, right?" She gave him an assessing glance. "Since a place like this—one that combines tradition and progress in such a magical blend—must have people fighting to secure a *tab-a tub*…er…" She waved at the handcrafted copper trays gleaming in the last rays of the sun and placed on foot-high, carved, solid mahogany bases.

"*Tubleyyah,*" he provided, picking up an incense stick, lighting it from the flame of an intricately worked brass lamp and placing it in the matching incense burner.

She gasped when the sweet-spicy scent of *ood*, his land's most valued incense, hit her. "Yeah, *that*…" A hot, short sound of pleasure escaped her, vibrating behind his ribs, shooting to his loins. The sensations spiked when her eyes narrowed on him with disapproval. "I bet the absence of customers is to accommodate you. And I bet I can't even imagine what that cost."

"Is your blood boiling at the misspent money?" His lips

spread, warmth and something he'd never felt towards a grown woman other than his mother—tenderness—humming in his.

She waved her hand. "Nah. This is not a hospital and it's your personal money—though you could do better with it… Oh, OK. My blood, while not boiling, is a few degrees above normal."

He shook his head in amazement. Everything she did and said was affecting him like an intravenous euphoric drug. "You'll be glad to know I exchange favors with the owner, not money."

"I won't ask what kind of favors."

He chuckled. "Very wise of you."

He knew she would have volleyed something if not for the arrival of more food. She sat watching a procession of waiters bearing one serving plate after another in arrested attention and vocal appreciation, all but licking her lips as their meal was served by a dozen waiters clearly thrilled to lavish their expertise on such guests as them.

Malek always demanded that only one served him and only when asked, but he'd ordered the full fanfare of service the restaurant was known for for her benefit, felt the spreading coolness of satisfaction in his chest at her delightfully flustered reaction at being waited on like that.

She went on to delight him further, not picking at her food or getting finicky about ingredients that experience told him foreigners balked at, at least at first exposure.

She attacked her meal with relish, kept reporting her experience with every mouthful. She enthused at the assorted grilled goat and sheep, including liver and brain, and the *kapsa*, the spiced rice with fried nuts and raisins, and the date wine. At trying *gahwa*, the cardamom Arabian coffee, her eyes widened at its bitterness, got even wider when he instructed her to drink it with the ultra-sweet chewy *agwa* dates. She went on to wash down a whole pack with a full carafe of coffee.

By the time *logmet el guadi* arrived, he was sure such a flat stomach couldn't hold any more food. But it did. She popped one of the crunchy, chewy golden spheres of fried dough dipped in thick syrup into her mouth and moaned. She washed it down with goat milk, murmuring "Sinful" and reaching for another one.

He didn't know why, but he thought this was the moment to tell her. "I cancelled the security checks."

She choked. He thumped her on the back to stop her coughing paroxysm. Her eyes glittered up at him from a bed of tears. "You mean into my dark past? Why did you do that?"

"Because I want to hear about it from your lips." In fact, he *needed* to. "And Janaan, this is not an interview."

"But you said—"

His lips twisted. "I would have said anything to get you to agree to come here with me."

"You conned me?" He only shrugged and held her eyes, unrepentant. At length she tossed her hair, sending the sunlit waterfall thudding down her back. "You deserve that I wolf down this mouth-watering food in silence."

And he guffawed. "You mean you still haven't?"

She popped another piece of *logmet el guadi* into her mouth and chewed defiantly.

He leaned closer, brushing her exposed forearm with his, took a piece himself, mimicking her actions.

After their *logmet el guadi* eating competition had emptied the plate, with her still looking up at the thirty-foot-high tented ceiling, he drawled, "You won't last. You can't be silent. Not with me."

She swung her eyes back to his, defiant, irritated—magnificent. Then she drawled back, "If this isn't work-related any more, why should I tell you anything?"

"No reason." He shrugged, knowing that his nonchalance was a flimsy act. Especially when he added, "Except for me."

For him. Was there a better incentive? Jay thought.

She sighed, wondered when she'd finally stumble back out of this fantasy dimension she'd spilled into the moment she'd plopped into his car and he'd materialized out of the darkness.

It had felt just as mystic as sharing this with him, the best meal—the best *experience*—of her life. Incense fumes shrouded them, echoes of past and future twining with distant live music, the reed-like lamenting *naay* weaving with the *oud*, the melancholy of the quarter-tones of the music deepening the feeling of unreality.

She leaned on one of those incredible cushions, resuming her surrender to this out-of-sanity, out-of-life encounter. "So—what do you want to hear? The highlights in bullet form?"

"We have all evening—as long as we want."

She watched him unfold his magnificent body, hers throbbing as he bent one endless leg on the floor, the other at the knee with his forearm resting there, like a sultan preparing to watch a show thousands had sweated their lives away to provide him with. He'd taken off his jacket and tie, rolled up his sleeves and undone his shirt. She'd been right. His body was that of a higher being. His beauty made her ache.

And he, this perfect creature, was asking her to reveal herself to him, of all people, when she'd never done so to anyone. It was one thing he'd find out her secrets from a security report, another that she'd tell him her story herself, in words she'd never tried to formulate—and see pity or even distaste forming in his eyes.

He reached out, ran a finger over the hands entwined tightly on her lap, startling her out of her chaos.

"Listen," she blurted out. "Just get on with your security checks. I'm sure your people will give you a far more accurate rundown of my life than I ever will."

"They would, if I wanted a background check, which I don't. I want to hear about you from you."

"There's not much to tell, really. It's all very boring."

"As boring as you've been so far? I'm certain it's an impossibility that you, or anything about you, can be boring."

What she'd thought about him earlier.

She fought to the surface, tried one last time. "I assure you a professionally gathered and written report will be far more entertaining."

He shook his head, dislodging a thick, glossy lock from his slicked-back mane. She thought she'd tell him anything for the privilege of smoothing it back. "Tell me, Janaan. Please."

It was the "please" that undid her.

"Oh, all right," she muttered. "But I'm shutting up at the first yawn."

He chuckled, did to her what she was dying to do to him and tucked back a lock of hair behind her ear, electrifying her. "If I yawn, it will be because in forty-eight hours I've only shut my eyes for the minutes it took for the accident to occur. You are the only thing keeping me awake."

"Oh… OK." With her last escape blocked she tried to think where to start, her heart bobbing in her throat.

He twined another lock of hair around two fingers, gave an almost imperceptible tug and whispered, "Start at the beginning."

He'd read her mind! Or maybe she was just too predictable.

But anyway, he'd given the only logical place to start.

She exhaled. "I was born twenty-eight years ago next month in Chicago to a twenty-year-old single mother. She never married, so I was an only child. With no family herself, it was all she could do to take care of an infant as she studied and worked as a nurse. When I was ten, she stopped working and we subsisted on unemployment pay. I guess even then she'd started the plunge into depression, that it was why she couldn't hold a job anymore. But she was only diagnosed with a major depressive disorder when I was fifteen. By then I was working in two part-time jobs to boost our meager income, had already jumped grades and had a scholarship to pre-med school. Once I entered med school, the scholarship lasted only one more year as I no longer qualified for it with my scores plummeting. By that time my mother was almost totally dependent as she started abusing alcohol and anything else she could lay her hands on. Soon we were in debt, and I had to work in any job I found just to keep us off the street…"

She stopped, groaned. God—she didn't have to tell him all that, not this explicitly, this intimately.

But she wanted to. For the first time in her life, she wanted… *needed* to share with another. With him…

What about him? He couldn't possibly want this level of personal detail imposed on him.

She ventured a look at him, whispered, "Sorry that you asked already? I told you it was boring. I neglected to mention it was pathetic too."

His hand wrapped around both of hers, squeezed, silencing her. "Don't. Depression is devastating to any family when any member is afflicted by it, but for it to be the mother, and for you to have had no family members to help you carry the ever-increasing burden! That you became in effect parent to a mother who was incapacitated by psychological illness, and at such a young age, is nothing short of heroic."

"Yeah, sure," she scoffed. "So heroic my mother kept plunging deeper, and I did less and less to pull her back as I kept getting busier. So heroic she ended up killing herself."

Silence crashed, splintering all around them, shredding her worse than the burst of relived anguish had.

She endured it for an overflowing moment, almost flinched when his fingers came beneath her chin, coaxing her face up to his. He insisted, moving closer, his body a protective barrier blockading her, warding off her torment, sympathy—*empathy*—blazing on his face. He'd known loss, helplessness to stop it, to reverse it. She knew it. And he was reaching out with the understanding that had been scarred into his own psyche, defusing her own guilt and agony.

"When?" His whisper was compassion itself.

She gulped, forced an answer. "T-two months ago."

"You're still in mourning." It was a statement.

She exhaled a tear-laden breath. "I've been mourning my mother's loss for over a decade. And the worst part was I never really got it—what was wrong with her. A friend once told me we take our psychological health for granted, that we never grasp how someone with a disorder feels. It's true. I lived with her suffering but, no matter what I go through in life, I'll never understand the prison of torment and despair she lived in. I can only hope she found peace. I still can't find any, can't stop thinking if I'd just listened to everyone's advice and put her in an institution, instead of insisting on taking care of her myself, they may have succeeded where I failed and pulled her back from that final act of desperation."

Her words petered out at the ferocity that appeared in his eyes. Or was it a rogue beam from the setting sun igniting the gold?

Then he spoke and there was no doubt what she'd seen.

"*Never* think that," he ground out. "You did everything beyond right and into outright self-sacrifice."

She shook her head, mortification sizzling in her cheeks. "There's no self-sacrifice in taking care of your family. She would have done the same for me if she'd been the healthy one and I had been the one with the affliction."

"It *was* self-sacrifice," he gritted, his eyes adamant, brooking no argument. "You didn't abandon her, someone who I'm sure people, starting with her doctors, labeled a lost cause to the care of strangers. You *knew* she wouldn't have been better off in an institution. As canny as addicts are, you knew they wouldn't have stopped her from abusing chemical substances. And she would have had the added torment of feeling abandoned by you. She would have suffered far more, before ending her life just the same. But most people would have gone that route, convincing themselves they were doing the best for their loved one while buying themselves a shot at an unburdened life. While I can't presume to condemn them for such a choice, I can't commend you enough for making the toughest one of all, and sticking with it. Your mother could have lived forty more years and you would have sacrificed your chance of a normal life, of building a family, for her."

She lowered eyes that felt about to burst. Not with remembering the ever-increasing burdens or the suffocating helplessness but with Malek's total understanding, with his assurance that she hadn't harmed her mother, who people *had* called a lost cause, by refusing to institutionalize her.

When she spoke, her tear-soaked voice was almost unintelligible with anguish. "You make it sound so noble, like I gave up my chance of building a family, when in reality I never thought of having one. It must have been my mother's disastrous experience tingeing my views of romantic involvements and domestic bliss."

"I find it impossible to believe hordes of men didn't try to change your mind," he drawled, his gaze burning down her body and back to her face.

Heat rose to her face, held for a second before flooding her body. She gave him a tremulous smile, desperate to lighten the mood. "Not sure about hordes, but some tried, the so-called serious ones, while letting it drop that a man didn't want a woman who came with such a burden."

"So only men in pursuit of flings didn't care about your situation," he bit off. "While men interested in a future and a family let you know they want you only as long as you came with no burdens."

She stared at him, stunned yet again at his laser-accurate insight. Then she shrugged. "I think any man has a right not to sacrifice the normality of his life for a stranger, to want an emotionally available—an available, *period*—wife."

His lips thinned. "I think any man who wants a woman to share his life must take her with her own better and worse, not demand or expect that she gets rid of her responsibilities to provide him with peace of mind."

To that ferocious declaration she had no answer.

She stared at him helplessly for a moment then exhaled.

"Actually, none of that really mattered after all. When my mother died, I figured out the most important reason why I'd never thought of having a family. One is supposed to live first before thinking of that. I realized I never have."

Silence thickened, along with the magma smoldering in his eyes. She felt it filling her lungs, slithering down her nerves, burning, besieging.

Then he finally drawled, "And to live, you came here. And instead of securing a lucrative job and enjoying the luxurious lifestyle Damhoor can offer someone of your assets and skills, you joined GAO. You have a singular definition of living, Janaan Latimer."

Her lips twitched in relief at his lighter tone. "Oh, there is method to my madness. I thought that to live I had to find out who I am. I thought I had to start with exploring the other half of my heritage. So I came here to find my father."

"Your father is Damhoorian?" She nodded and he shook his head in amazement. Then he drawled, his voice dropping to fathomless reaches, "Janaan of the ceaseless surprises." He looked at her for a long moment, as if he were studying a multi-faceted gem. Then he cocked his head, making her heart tilt to the same angle inside her chest. "When did you find out about him?"

"All my life," she said. "It was him who named me, though he couldn't give me his name. He was the only man in my mother's life, and though her psyche must have been fragile to start with, I think his loss and my birth were the catalysts that initiated her descent. She fell in love with him when she was here as an exchange student, but it turned out he was married, had children already and his family forbade him to take her as a second wife. Or to acknowledge me. He visited us a few times when I was growing up, phoned frequently, always telling me how much he loved me, how sorry was he couldn't be with us. He helped financially by paying into a trust fund. Towards the end he called more, saying he was hoping to finally have us with him. Then he suddenly stopped calling. A few months later my mother killed herself. I think it was giving up on him that made her give up on life."

She paused for breath, the breath the intensity of his gaze was knocking out of her lungs. She needed it, to get it all out, to lay her innermost self bare before him. "So after all the investigations into my mother's death had been concluded, I felt like the foundation of my life had been yanked from underneath me and I was dangling in a vacuum. I guess I needed a new foundation, and just five days ago I made a decision to use the money he'd saved for me to come here, find my roots so to speak, in the country I lived my life dreaming I'd one day live in, with a miraculously healed mother, a father and siblings. Problem was, I found out the reason for my father's silence. He was dead. And my half-siblings understandably don't want to know about me..."

He took her hand when she faltered, enveloped it, infusing her with his power, giving her the strength to finish her story.

She went on, "But I fell in love with this land the moment I set foot here, really began to understand the hold it had on my father. I was torn about leaving, wanted to stay, to try to get to know him by getting to know the culture that had ruled his life and choices. But stay to do what? I wasn't up to applying for a job, didn't even want one. Then practically on my way to the airport just two days ago, I stumbled on GAO's ad, asking for volunteers. And it was like a prayer answered and a dream come true in one. I always wanted to join GAO, but my responsibility to my mother tied me to one place with a regular job. Now I no longer have to provide for her, I'm doing what I always wanted while also getting my chance to stay here. And with the money my father left me I can afford to stay here as a volunteer for at least a couple of months, quite comfortably." She gave him another wavering smile. "So that's my whole life story, till the moment you drove me off the road."

Malek stared at her, his heart staggering in his chest.

He'd never known such honesty, such unadorned recounting of such heart-wrenching events. He'd never known that such compassion towards those who'd ruined one's life could exist. She'd given them all forbearance and forgiveness, when she didn't extend half the mercy to herself. The mother who'd deprived her of her childhood and youth, of normality and peace, the father who'd abandoned her to the custody of a damaged mother while he'd lavished his all on his legitimate children, those who had taken it all and refused to even recognize her as their blood kin.

How he felt the need to avenge her, to erase her suffering.

Not that she acknowledged she'd suffered or sacrificed. She'd cited her ordeals matter-of-factly, and now they were over she was moving on to the next chore. Joining GAO so she'd spend heaven knew how much more of her life giving to others, with no expectation of pay or thanks or even acknowledgement.

She'd already made him feel what he'd never felt before, but this insight into the depths of her suffering and strength increased her appeal a thousandfold.

And it went beyond passion. Beyond compassion. She moved him, shook him. On every level.

Nothing was left in him but the need to comfort her, connect with her, erase all damage, imbue her with all he had of healing and succor. It was no use resisting any more.

He reached for her, watched her eyes widening, her flushed lips parting on a tiny cry of surprise and, he knew, surrender, as he swept her over his body, folded her in his lap and contained her in a hug. It felt as if she had been made to fit within him, as if he had been made to wrap around her.

"Malek…"

He had no idea if she'd gasped his name, or if he'd felt it reverberating in her mind. He'd never realized his name was so beautiful. It was, on her lips, in her mind. Where he wanted it to be, always.

He drove a hand into the depth of that mink-soft mane, his fingers combing through it soothingly, his other one pressing her face into his neck as he murmured to her in Arabic, what she made him feel, how he wanted to comfort her.

Feeling her in his arms, her hot resilience unraveling him one nerve at a time, he knew he could stop himself from taking the comforting deeper into communion, flesh to flesh, lips to lips, as easily as he could stop breathing.

He leaned back against the wall, taking her unresisting body with him, raising her with an arm around her waist, bringing her face level with his, saw in her eyes a reflection of his fever, in her trembling lips his admission of defeat. A gentle hand behind her head urged her to close the gap, end the aching, brought the sweetness of her breath scorching him, the first touch with her lips half a gasp away… And his cell-phone rang.

The single-note ring went through him like a skewer.

It had an even more spectacular effect on her. She lurched, twisted off him, gasping, scrambling away from him, ending up in a heap on the opposite collection of cushions.

They stared at each other for a suspended moment. All he wanted to do was to storm up to his feet, crush his phone beneath them, then swoop down to scoop her in his arms, claim that kiss, claim her, then sweep her back to his place…

"Will you please answer that?" Her voice wobbled as her hands shook over her hair and clothes, smoothing away the signs of their surrender to insanity. "That ringtone is drilling a hole in my head. And it seems whoever it is won't give up."

"They will have to. Janaan…" he started, needing to fix this, continue it more slowly, or to end it at once. He didn't know which. Or anything.

She cut through his words. "Please—just answer it. I doubt you give your number to just anyone. This may be an emergency."

He acknowledged her logic. And that he had lost his. Probably irrevocably.

With a last glance at her he muttered a curse, retrieved his phone from his discarded jacket. He almost punched his finger through the answer button. *"W'Ullahi ya Saeed..."*

And the sworn promise of retribution only froze on his lips with Saeed's first urgent words.

CHAPTER FIVE

"WHAT IS IT?"

Jay heard the shaken question spilling from her lips. She wondered if he'd heard it, understood it. She barely could.

Even ten minutes after the phone call had interrupted her headlong plunge into his arms and insanity, she still felt Malek's body beneath hers, every sinew and bone and muscle driving into hers, liquefying her, still felt his breath scorching her face, his warm, tough fingers in her hair, until she was certain there'd be marks singed into her skin, carved into her flesh everywhere he'd touched.

She bit her lips. The almost kiss was what burned her most. Her lips were swollen, chafing, and only abusing them seemed to lessen the throbbing, curb the mad desire to obey their screaming, go bury them into the power and hard, virile beauty of his exposed neck and chest.

It didn't help that every now and then through his call, his eyes had fallen on her, drenching her in his simmering hunger and frustration. All her nerves jangled an all-out response that had only subsided to endurable levels when he'd torn his eyes away and progressed to the next phone call.

She'd waited for him to end the last one to ask her question. But he only gave her an absent glance and started another one. Either he hadn't heard her, or she'd been as incoherent as she'd thought. *Or* he didn't think it a priority to answer her. She didn't understand any of his barked colloquial Damhoorian, but it was enough to see the urgency in his face and body to know that something was wrong. Dreadfully wrong.

The certainty overrode her agitation, focusing her away from her own turmoil. There *was* an emergency. Now, if he'd only deign to tell her what it was!

He finally snapped his phone shut, looked down at her, his face a grim mask. Then he turned on his heel and strode away.

After a stunned moment she grabbed her bag and heaved herself to her feet, found him coming back with an older man in tow.

She froze at the urgency in his eyes, melted at the solicitousness in his hand on her bare arm.

"Janaan, this is Adnan El-Haddad, the proprietor, and he will be honored to serve you every meal from now on, whether from his establishment or any other you desire, in-house or delivered to your doorstep. And wherever you want to go and whatever you want to do in the kingdom, I'll leave my personal driver and my top aide at your disposal, day and night, to fulfill your every demand." He nodded to the man, waited for him to bow to her and turn away before he added, his voice plunging to bass reaches, "I would have given anything to have more time with you, but I am forced to leave you in my men's care to attend to urgent business."

"Will you, please, tell me what is going on?" Her demand was out, ragged, pleading, just as a sobering thought hit her. "If it's *not* personal..." Though what she'd give to be of help if it was!

His brow furrowed. "Would that it were, Janaan. No—it's a catastrophe in progress. The torrential rain that has swept our neighbor, Ashgoon, from where I just returned this morning, has hit Mejbel, a coastal region on Damhoor's borders. Damage is spreading and the numbers of the injured, missing or dead are rising. I have to fly there immediately to organize rescue efforts, damage control and medical relief." He wrapped one arm around her shoulders, gathered her to him in a hug full of apology and assurance. "I'll be in contact as soon as everything is under control."

With one final glance, crowded with so many emotions that she almost grabbed his face to fathom them, he turned her away from him, relinquished his hold on her gradually, ending with his fingers sliding off hers, making her feel she'd plummet down some abyss the moment he let go. Then he turned and strode away.

She stood transfixed, watching his powerful figure receding.

Then she shook off her daze and raced after him, vaguely registering the sound of approaching thunder. Once outside, she realized what it was.

A gigantic helicopter was landing in the parking lot, at least a hundred feet in length, its white fuselage giving off an eerie glow in the fading twilight and the subdued orange streetlights, the red crescent insignia on its side proclaiming it a medical transport.

Malek's men raced to pull the door near its tail downwards, releasing in-built steps, and he rushed towards it, unbending even in the storm of the rotors' unabated spinning.

In seconds he'd be on board, would fly away!

"*Malek*."

He swung around at her frantic cry.

His face taut, he waved his men away as she ran towards him, struggling against the buffeting wind. He shouted over the din of the helicopter, "Janaan, I can't—"

"Take me with you," she gasped across his protest. His face froze before closing on instant and adamant rejection. Before he articulated it, she went on, "I *am* an emergency doctor. Who better to have on your medical relief team?"

"*La ya* Janaan." She started to protest, and he gripped her arm and led her away from the chopper. Once far enough away from the noise, he looked down at her. "From early reports, conditions there are horrendous, and they will get worse before they get better."

"So? I don't see that stopping you."

"It is my duty and my responsibility."

"Ditto. I'm a doctor here, too. Helping the injured *is* the job description. Or am I supposed to join humanitarian missions only if they present no danger? *If* such missions exist."

"How about starting with something less dangerous?"

"Like what? A drive on a satin-smooth and empty highway in broad daylight? We found out how safe *that* was this morning."

His lips twitched. The next moment they were uncompromising, however, making her doubt she'd seen that sign of unwilling humor. "You're staying here, Janaan, and that's final."

She folded her arms across her chest. "And what should I do while people who need my medical skill drown and die? Stay in my hotel, preferably under my bed? With my luck, Damhoor will be hit with its first earthquake and I'll be crushed underneath it."

He closed his eyes, visibly wrestling with his impatience. "Janaan, I don't have time to argue—"

"Then don't. Let me hop inside that chopper with you and let's go do our job."

"*Your* job is with GAO. Wait for *their* mission." With that he turned away, his dismissal freezing her blood.

He'd just taken a couple of strides when she called out to him. He turned to scowl at her, the lights from the restaurant casting shadows on his annoyed, unyielding, brutally handsome face.

"Just to let you know, I *am* joining GAO's mission—the one I'm sure they'll organize to the afflicted region. If they don't, I'll fly there on my own. I'm sure any humanitarian effort will want my services. Maybe I'll see you there." Then she turned and ran towards the car he'd provided for her use.

Less than a heartbeat later both her arms were clamped inexorably by his hands. He couldn't have moved so quickly!

But he *was* at her back, swamping her with his heat and presence, muttering to himself, *"Ya Gawwi men hadi'l aneedah."*

That she got. She guessed. He was calling on God to help him endure her stubbornness.

Sure enough, he growled, "You stubborn firebrand." Then he

marched her towards the helicopter, his body shielding her from the buffeting that had almost swept her away when she'd first approached it. He took the four steps up in one bound then bent to her, scooped her up as if she weighed nothing.

As one of his men jumped inside after them and drew up the door, her heart slammed around inside her chest.

Malek still had his arm around her when minutes ago she'd been certain she'd never see him again. The fact that he was taking her with him was too much!

Her legs wobbled as he guided her through a cargo bay with dozens of folded seats lining its sides and towering crates marked as medical and relief supplies. In the next section, she saw many closed compartments flanking a bay that contained over a dozen emergency stations.

She finally located her voice and croaked, "What's this thing? A flying hospital?"

He only gave her an inscrutable look as he steered her forward to a four-seat pressurized passenger compartment. Four men came out of what had to be the cockpit, and from what she knew of aircrews they had to be a pilot, a copilot, a navigator, and a flight engineer. She saw the respect with which they treated Malek, knew they considered him a superior—no, far more.

She had a vague idea that Damhoor had thousands of people related to the royal family who were of incredibly varying levels of importance and power. From the men's reaction, it seemed Malek was fairly high on the royal food chain. And she couldn't *believe* it hadn't occurred to her to ask exactly what his position was! The man she'd shared so many firsts with.

Her first time as a first responder. Her first sharing of her life story with another. Her first plunge into total loss of control. So many world-shaking experiences. *Her* world, that was. And she knew nothing about him beyond his name, that he was a doctor and a sheikh, and obviously an important one.

Soon he sent the crew back to the cockpit, seated her and

himself, fastened their seat belts, and the chopper took off without so much as a tremor.

As they soared, she felt Malek's eyes on her. She tore her gaze away from the breathtaking sight of the glittering city receding beneath them in the deepening night and turned to him.

"In answer to your earlier question," he drawled, "this chopper is the next best thing to a real flying hospital—it can land in Mejbel where there's no landing strip. It's an Mi-26MS helicopter, a Medevac version built to my specifications. It features an OR, an ER, an IC and sixteen stretcher stations. It's carrying its top load of seventy thousand pounds of medical and relief supplies but, once unloaded, it can hold over a hundred people in the cargo bay."

Before she could process the staggering resources and power that had secured such a giant and its equipment and supplies, his hands clamped her shoulders, turned her to him, burning more palm prints into her flesh. "So are you happy now your ruse worked?"

"What ruse?" She gaped at him.

"So cunningly giving me a choice between you being in danger with me or without me, knowing which way I'd jump."

"I did no such thing!" she cried indignantly. "I was just telling you I didn't need your approval to do my job!"

His gaze went on and on, boring into her, until she felt he could read her every thought. *And* that he would let his accusation go unwithdrawn and her protest unacknowledged.

Then he shook his head with a half amused, half incredulous sound. "I can't believe I'm saying this, but I believe you."

"Oh, I'm just thrilled! How lovely to have a slur withdrawn by such a near insult."

His lips twisted. "Where's the slur in the fact that females reach their goals through manipulation? And where's the insult in my belief in your shocking deficiency in that basic skill?"

"You'd better watch it before you have an offensiveness overdose and slip into a chauvinistic coma," she scoffed.

He barked a laugh. "If either can assure me of some solid sleep, I'd welcome it."

She seethed at the unfairness of it all, that one person should be endowed with all that, that he'd probably make real offensiveness and chauvinism look delicious.

He adjusted his seat backwards, sprawled in a more comfortable position. "I hope you won't think me more of an uncouth miscreant if I sleep until we reach our destination."

She again noticed fatigue straining his face and dulling his eyes, felt contrite that she'd been the reason he'd gone an extra twelve hours without sleep, barely stopped herself from offering her bosom, or any part of her for more comfort.

"Please, go ahead. I'll shut up now." But before she did... "But, uh, you do believe I wasn't being manipulative, don't you?"

"I wouldn't have said I did if I didn't." His eyelids swept down until ridiculously thick lashes brushed razor-sharp cheekbones, his voice growing thicker and even more intoxicating with impending sleep. "What you did worked nevertheless. You may soon wish it hadn't, though. I'm keeping you within three feet of me all through our time in Mejbel. And this, Janaan, is non-negotiable."

Before she could say anything to that, he pulled her to him, bringing her head resting on *his* bosom, probably frying her speech centers permanently. Before his breathing fell into the regular cadence of deep sleep he murmured into her temple, "Get some sleep, Janaan. I foresee some harrowing times ahead. We'd better stock up on stamina."

The last things Malek remembered before he surrendered to exhaustion was soaking up Janaan's softness and warmth, filling his lungs with her scent and feeling his every nerve humming with the pleasure of her nearness.

The very things whose absence woke him up now.

He opened his eyes to the darkened cabin, felt she wasn't there, not even on board, even before he felt that they'd landed.

Groggy with the coma-like sleep he'd plunged into, he snatched off his seat belt, heaved himself up to his feet, an unreasoning fear riding him that she'd somehow disappeared while he'd slept, that something had happened to her under his very nose.

As wakefulness chased away doubt, he was certain she'd just disembarked when they'd landed, not wanting to disturb him. *And* probably showing him she wouldn't abide by his three-feet decree. He clamped his jaw. Oh, she would abide by it.

He might have succumbed to his need to have her with him, but he was keeping her within those three feet or less until the crisis was over. He was sending her back, no matter what she said, if he felt he couldn't keep her a hundred percent safe, or if he felt her unable to deal with the reality of the situation.

He stepped out of the helicopter. He had some aides he had to blast for not waking him up as soon as they'd arrived with the crisis in progress and for letting her out of the helicopter.

Then the first thing his eyes fell on a hundred feet away was her lithe figure glowing in his helicopter's lights, her hair blowing around her and everything drained out of him but the need to be by her side.

He exhaled remnants of anxiety, inhaled steadiness for the coming ordeals then bounded across the distance separating them.

Jay stood staring at the squadron of helicopters that was landing around theirs and wondered if she could stop being stunned at the extent of resources Malek commanded.

The area around them had been turned in part into a camp for the reception of displaced people and in part into a field hospital. She was sure everything had materialized in the two hours it had taken them to get there, at his orders.

Suddenly coin-sized drops of water splashed down on her.

Before she could move, it was as if floodgates had burst and there was no point in rushing away any more—or at all. She'd probably spend the next days soaking wet anyway. To make it worse, it was clear the heatwave had broken. With a vengeance.

She shuddered, raised her eyes to the sky, and even in the darkness saw the bloated clouds that promised a ceaseless deluge, and hoped Malek had estimated the site of their relief operation correctly, that it was on high enough ground not to join the afflicted areas in their watery fate.

"What have I told you about moving about without me?"

She jumped with a yelp before she subsided against him as he wrapped her in his jacket. Another thing she'd never get used to—his stealth. How could such a big man move so quietly?

He towed her to the nearest tent. "You're soaked, and you weren't dressed for this to start with."

"Neither are you. And then I started the day in a heatwave, lost my jacket..." *Stop, stop, you're babbling.*

And was it any wonder? Her eyes couldn't tear themselves away from the sight of his clinging wet clothes showcasing the majesty of his chest, abdomen and thighs in distressing detail.

God—she was ogling him. She'd never done that, never felt the painful urge, or any urge at all, to tear a man's clothes off him. And for her to feel this way here, now... It was crazy!

She busied herself with wringing her hair out as another crew member provided them with towels and waterproof, phosphorescent yellow uniforms like those everyone in the relief effort was wearing. She hurried into one of the still empty treatment compartments, dried herself and dressed, only then noticing that he'd ordered her a uniform indicating she was a doctor. "*Tubeeb*" was written in big letters above "*Doctor*", front and back, plus the red crescent, indicating medical services.

She rushed out to find one of Malek's men, Saeed, a huge, intimidating-looking man, the one she was now certain was the top aide he'd bequeathed her when he'd intended to leave her behind, and who'd been the one who'd accompanied them on the flight, taking Malek aside for a short, tense tête-à-tête.

Malek turned with a deep frown, reached out a silent hand to her. She rushed to take it.

"We're holding a strategy planning meeting," he murmured as she hurried beside him to another compartment where there were five men and one woman. They were gathered around a table with maps spread on it.

As soon as Malek entered they sprang up straight. The closest rushed over and kissed Malek's shoulder.

Was that a kiss on the cheek going astray, with the man being so much shorter than Malek?

Malek cut through her musings. "No time for standing on ceremony." Ceremony? This was the way to greet sheikhs here? Not that it was time to begin her education in the land's customs. Malek's taut admonition sent them all backing away. "A quick introduction is in order, though. Everyone, Dr Janaan Latimer is an emergency doctor who just this morning saved a citizen from a car crash. She's an affiliate of GAO and she is generously volunteering even more services to our kingdom in its time of need." Then he turned to her. "Janaan, let me introduce your colleagues in the relief effort. Dr Hessuh El-Etaibi…"

The striking dark-haired woman, who to Jay's surprise was unveiled and dressed like the men, came forward and shook her hand with a smile full of genuine charm and interest.

She would have loved to have exchanged a more substantial greeting with her, but Malek swept her into a succession of lightning-quick introductions, giving her colleagues' names but nothing about their functions.

It was over in one minute flat then Malek said, "Reports?"

"Those who escaped when the flashflood forged a new path down El Shamekh mountain," Dr Essam said, "described it as a wall of water that came crashing down on them. They say their villages, which lie at its foot, here and here…" he pointed a baton on the map "...have been wiped out."

"Our meteorologists estimate that over twenty centimeters of rain have fallen over the last twelve hours," Khaled El-Mussri, who looked and acted like some military type, said. "They predict more over the next seventy-two hours. Even in the areas that weren't hit as hard, the water choked arterial roads and blocked them with waist-high water."

"The timing, with night falling, proved a huge complication," Hessuh said. "Then power lines went down and the blackout compounded the chaos. The local police and emergency services are paralyzed. The new mobile health units are either inundated by water or by people. We're the first outside help to arrive."

Malek took in all the information and exhaled. "The army has been mobilized but with the roads inaccessible, soldiers must hike for hours then use inflatable boats to reach the disaster areas. Every helicopter in the kingdom is on its way, but right now we are the only chance the victims have for immediate help."

Essam shook his head. "There's nothing we can do right now. The wind alone can bring the lighter helicopters down, and the zero visibility makes any rescue attempt before dawn futile."

Malek straightened. She felt everyone in the compartment shrinking. She shivered, but it wasn't with cold.

"Those people will *not* wait till dawn," Malek snarled. "We're repeating the drill we conducted in Ashgoon. Search-and-rescue teams will conduct continuous aerial surveys using the floodlights being fitted to the helicopters as we speak. They will pick up victims, deliver them to our medical team, then go back for more. When every single injured or stranded person has been rescued, we'll continue the search for the missing and the dead. I am not leaving one person unaccounted for. Is that clear?"

There were unanimous nods, hers the most vigorous.

She knew that with him in charge, every life would be

fought for and if not salvaged then honored, with everything humanly possible.

She ran after him as he distributed assignments to his team leaders.

"On which team will you be?" she gasped.

Malek looked down on her. "My helicopter is the only one equipped for both rescue and critical care. I'll be on both."

She speeded up to keep up with him. "And since I'm to be kept within three feet of you, so will I."

CHAPTER SIX

MEJBEL WAS A collection of small towns and villages, one of the few places in Damhoor where the modern world hadn't taken over. Right now it was water that had.

Jay looked down from her window, failed again to imagine what the people had felt when water had invaded their homes, swept away their lives as they'd known it. Her heart seemed to be in a state of perpetual contraction as she saw nothing but roofs jutting out of the water, with higher areas in the path of the torrent becoming instant burial grounds. They'd rescued people who'd wept about how they'd failed to dig out their loved ones from the landslides with nothing to use but their bare hands.

It had been nine hours of unceasing flying between the most affected areas and the relief operation site. Their helicopter alone had rescued six hundred and eighty-two stranded and injured people. The rest of the chopper fleet had contributed a total flying time of six hundred hours, each rescuing over three hundred people. They'd rescued people from everywhere they'd escaped to—rooftops, trees, upper floors of makeshift shelters in schools, public buildings and mosques. At six a.m. their camp and field hospital had been filled beyond capacity with around forty thousand people vying for shelter and treatment.

On the way to the camp they'd treated those whose condition had been critical. With another doctor, whose specialty she didn't catch, and four trauma nurses along, they treated everything from concussion to severe crush injuries to near-drownings. They resuscitated dozens, stabilized more, lost three casualties, two to drowning and one to electrocution. Malek had flitted between his medical and co-ordinating roles, making her head spin just watching his sheer energy and efficiency.

The local police informed them that they'd issued warnings to two hundred thousand people in the areas predicted to be hit hardest to evacuate their residences. Most hadn't complied.

And who could blame them? Leave everything they had behind and go where?

She knew all had a tragedy to relate but in the deluge of faces it was one family, whose father spoke good English, who gave her a close-up look at the heart-wrenching losses suffered. And they were one of the lucky families who hadn't lost a member or been separated in the chaos.

The woman, Samira, clutched her three children to her as she sobbed into her husband's chest. He clutched her in turn while Jay tended the severe gash he'd sustained down his back as he'd struggled to save his family.

"We worked for ten years for our house and shop and they were gone in ten minutes," Jaaber lamented. "We lost the car, the clothes, the children's paintings—our pictures—our memories. We lost everything. This has to be a punishment from Ullah."

Jay insisted it wasn't, that tragedies just happened, that you bounced back as long as you had breath left in you.

When she had used up all her arguments, she said, "Well, Jaaber, you have your family. Look around and see how many people don't have theirs and count your blessings."

This seemed to calm him down. From then on he and his wife were of great help, tending other victims' needs.

GAO had arrived on their heels in more helicopters provided by Malek, and he co-ordinated with them about the transfer of fresh water and more food and medicine for the survivors. And more body bags for the dead.

It was dawn now. At least, her watch said so. The sky was weeping solid sheets of water from an impenetrable barrier of clouds. They were now returning to the affected areas after depositing their last helicopter load of refugees at the camp. It was by now doubtful they'd find more. Alive, that was.

"Pilot—three o'clock, from my position," she heard Malek barking into his walkie-talkie over the clamor of the chopper and the downpour. "A half-submerged red car beneath a palm." He turned to Saeed. "We'll lift the car, see if there are any survivors once it's back on dry land."

Saeed nodded and ran to fulfill his boss's directives.

Moving the huge palm off the car took over thirty minutes, and it took as long to secure the car for the aerial ride.

Once they'd landed the car, Malek, Saeed, Dr Rafeeq, the navigator and the flight engineer jumped out to unhook the cables so the chopper could land.

She jumped down and raced to Malek's side. He scowled down at her, his face frightening in the harsh floodlights from the helicopter. "Get back in there, Janaan."

"I'm here to do my job."

"Do it inside."

"I have nothing to do inside—no patients, remember?"

He clamped his teeth on an expletive then turned and ordered his men away from the car. It looked like crumpled foil around the victims. He reached for the driver through the compressed space of the pulverized window and Jay ran to the passenger seat to examine the woman. A palpation of her carotid artery gave her an instant verdict. The woman was dead. Long dead.

Hope bled out of her in booming heartbeats as she raised stinging eyes to Malek. He raised his eyes at the same moment, the same bleak diagnosis in his. Dead.

Then she noticed something in the backseat. Was this…?

"Malek," she cried out. "There's someone in the back seat."

Malek raced around to her side, bent to peer into the crack where the tree had flattened the top of the car into the back seat. "You're right. Let's hope it's a child." Her eyes swung up in shock. He elaborated. "An adult would have been crushed. Being smaller might prove the casualty's only chance."

"But the car had been submerged!"

"Half-submerged. The man and woman didn't drown. The impact of the tree killed them." Then he bellowed for a crowbar.

It was in his hands in seconds and he pried the compressed space widely enough for Jay's smaller arm to reach inside and feel for the passenger.

After a minute she pulled back, gasping, her eyes filling. "It *is* a child. A boy. He's alive. Barely. *God*, Malek, please, get him out of there. We have to save him."

Malek squeezed her arm, his orders bringing his men with chainsaws. Then the nightmare of extracting the boy from the car began. An hour-long nightmare.

As minutes ticked by Jay felt like she would burst with frustration, feeling the boy's life ebbing with every passing second and unable to do anything about it. If not for Malek's steadying grip and presence, she would have screamed.

Then the top of the car was torn off and she and Malek pounced on the boy, a little angel of around seven, with silky black hair and fine features, the olive of his skin fading along with his life force.

Trembling, she fitted him with a cervical collar and Malek an oxygen mask. With a shared nod they carried him to the gurney. In the periphery of her vision she saw Malek's men extracting the dead man and woman from their death trap. Her insides twisted.

They took the boy inside and Malek barked, "Rafeeq, ready OR, Alyaa, prepare CT, Lobna, expose the patient as we work."

His eyes slammed into Jay, who'd just snapped on gloves, and without words each took a chore.

Just as she finished intubating the boy and started positive pressure ventilation, she heard Saeed's subdued words in Malek's ear.

Malek nodded as he finished hooking the boy to the cardiac monitor and oximeter, reported his findings. "Pulse 45, BP 70 over 30, oxygen 80 percent."

Lobna finished cutting the boy's clothes off and Jay pounced on him for a quick survey.

"No gross injuries," she muttered. "God, Malek, his coma and vital signs depression are probably due to brain injury."

Malek gave a grim nod, then let out a heavy exhalation. "They were his mother and father, Shabaan Abul-Hamd and Kareemah El-Swaifi. He is Adham."

Adham. Black. Like his silken hair and lashes.

She compressed her lips against pity, calling on the hard-earned distancing techniques she'd developed through years of discipline so she'd be of use to her patients, to her mother, letting herself feel devastation only when they no longer needed her. But they'd never stopped needing her and she'd had her distance program perpetually on.

Then she'd met Malek, then all this had happened and she could now barely locate it, let alone turn it on.

She gritted her teeth, swung her gaze up, groping for Malek's support.

He gave it, his voice when he spoke, his words, their intensity and import, almost breaking her control. "He won't share their fate. Not if we have anything to say about it."

A cold fist in her chest melted, scalded her. Yes. *Please.*

He turned to Adham and she jumped to join him in a thorough exam. They found no signs of internal injuries. That supported the head-trauma scenario.

Raising his blood pressure to raise his cerebral perfusion took on a new urgency. She announced her intervention method as she implemented it. "I'm giving Adham a 250 c.c. saline bolus. Will continue with a rapid drip for two more liters."

Malek nodded, making her heart bob in her chest with the approval in his eyes. Then he rose as soon as Rafeeq walked back to them. "Rafeeq, give me vitals every five minutes. I'll check preparations."

"I'll get a GCS," she called out after him, gliding her hands over the boy, translating his reflexes. Soon she called out her bleak assessment to Malek. "It's six. One-three-two."

Malek strode back to them, frowning. "Status?"

"BP 80 over 40, pulse 50, oxygen at 85 percent," Rafeeq said.

Malek's huff was eloquent. "Let's see what's keeping our measures from working properly."

He pushed the trolley to the CT machine. In seconds he had Adham inside it, with both Jay and Rafeeq making sure his oxygen and fluid supplies weren't interrupted.

As Malek put the machine in motion, a terrible realization gripped her.

"Malek—he also has a unilaterally dilated right pupil, with ipsilateral third cranial nerve paralysis. Do you think…?"

Malek grimaced. "His brain is herniating."

Jay jerked at his corroboration of her new-formed fear.

Her own brain felt about to burst. Adham might have to have a craniotomy to relieve the building pressure inside his skull and if they didn't have a surgeon qualified for such hazardous surgery, they would have to reduce Adham's intracranial pressure long enough to reach someone qualified to operate on him.

With unspoken co-operation they applied the measures to do just that, with Jay administering mannitol and Malek hyperventilating him.

She finished as he did and muttered, "If it doesn't work…"

He sighed. "We have to give him a chance to stabilize without surgical intervention. He may not need a craniotomy."

His words failed to bolster her. The doubt tingeing them made her heart itch, constrict. *C'mon Adham, please.*

Malek turned those potent eyes on her, intent on absorbing her agitation. "If he doesn't respond, we'll operate."

"Wh-who'll operate?" she croaked.

"I will," he said simply.

He was a *surgeon*?

And he claimed *she* was "of the ceaseless surprises"?

She couldn't *believe* she hadn't realized he had to be a surgeon when he'd asked Rafeeq to prepare OR! Soggy cotton *had* replaced her brain. And if he talked about performing a craniotomy in their circumstances with such assurance, he wasn't just any surgeon but a superior one.

And she believed he was. Believed he could do anything, was delirious with gratitude he was there to do it.

She only hoped he'd let her assist him. She'd trained for six months in trauma surgery before changing her direction for a predictable specialty, shift-wise, for her mother's needs.

The need to lean on him was overwhelming. As if he felt her need, he drew her back against him as they watched CT images forming on the monitor. She breathed in his scent, absorbed his steadying power, her mind racing to process the opacities pinpointing hemorrhage and diffuse tissue swelling.

Then his voice broke over her, filled with compassion and somberness as he discussed diagnosis and possibilities.

The CT machine whirred to a stop and Malek reversed the gliding table. As he saved and printed out the results, Jay examined Adham, reassessing.

A minute later she raised her eyes to Malek's and choked, "The deficit's increased. Malek, you have to operate."

Malek held her gaze, her hand. "We will." He searched her eyes. "You do want to assist me, don't you?"

Malek moved the suction probe to and fro over the subdural hematoma. "A bit more irrigation here, Janaan."

But she was already gently irrigating in conjunction with his suction to loosen the clot.

By now he knew he didn't need to give her directions. She was a flawless, intuitive assistant. The best he'd ever had.

They now worked together as if they'd worked together every day of their lives, handling the most delicate part, removing clots that had collected between the inner and outer coverings of Adham's brain, then delving deeper into the brain to remove clots formed there and closing bleeding arteries.

"Craniotomy is the worst emergency surgery there is, right?" Jay whispered.

So she wasn't as firm as she appeared to be. He snapped a look at her and her reddened eyes discharged another chain reaction in his chest. No, not firm, disintegrating with worry and pity but holding up nevertheless, functioning at optimum, to be his support, and Adham's. It was a marvel that she could.

She might be used to trauma, but trauma *surgery* was something else altogether. And then she was right. Among all the gory, horrific procedures, opening the skull, exposing the brain, took the cake. And when it was a child, his own personal worst-case scenario, and not any child but one who didn't have a family to wake up to, a home to go back to…

He gritted his teeth, gave her the support she needed, channeled all the sympathy into his healing abilities.

He could still do nothing about the brain tissue lacerations. It was time to close up.

As he started closure, Jay suddenly talked again, her voice an impeded rasp. "He's going to be OK now, isn't he?"

He raised his eyes to hers, felt confident enough to say, "He's so young, his brain will get over the insult."

"And what about—about…?"

He had to spare her articulating her anxiety. "I'll take care of him. I'll take care of them all. I promise you."

He could only see her heavenly eyes, kindling with a warmth

that spread right to his bones, glittering with unshed tears. One escaped to darken her mask when she gave a vigorous nod.

They fell silent again as they concluded Adham's procedure. Jay drew the skin over the craniotomy, stapling it and applying dressings while Rafeeq terminated anesthesia.

As their assistants took Adham to IC, Malek took Janaan's arm, escorted her to the soiled compartment. She swayed against him. He helped her take off her surgical garments. She was pale, her lips blue, her eyes raw, tearing at his insides even harder than the ordeals they'd been through. He took her hands in his, a pressure building inside him. He had to release it.

He cupped her cheek. "Janaan, I can't express how thankful to God I am that he sent you to my people in their hour of need, and to me to stand beside me in this trial."

Before he surrendered to the urge to complete the madness he'd started back in Adnan's restaurant, he closed his eyes then turned on his heel and rushed to plunge himself into the distraction of the ongoing crisis.

Jay stood there, her heart pounding so hard it shook her.

It took Lobna asking if she was all right to shake her out of her trance. Jay blinked, asked the one thing she could think of, "What kind of surgeon is Ma—is Dr Aal Hamdaan?"

Lobna gaped at her as if she'd asked her what kind of vegetable he was. "He is not."

It was Jay's turn to gape. "He's not a surgeon?"

The woman gave an apologetic smile, her eyes brimming with curiosity. "Sorry, but I don't use English beyond medical terms much. I mean he's not just a surgeon. Sheikh Malek is our Health Minister, the best Damhoor has ever had, or will ever have."

CHAPTER SEVEN

JAY STOOD OUTSIDE her tent, surveying the hundreds of multi-sized, waterproofed ones lined up on the arid hill. Something was different about them today. They were dry.

She looked up and the sun zapped her eyes with its 8 a.m. glare. She snapped them away, looked around the waking camp, *"sabaah'l khayr"*, an automatic good morning, on her lips as she greeted the people passing by.

Things had slowed down in the past three days, with the rain stopping, the injured either back on their feet or at least getting better, and all the displaced people getting used to their temporary but very adequate accommodation until a permanent replacement for their losses was devised.

It had been a week since it had all started. And during that time, when the constant toil and preoccupation had allowed her moments of coherence, she'd only been able to think of one thing.

Malek. And the fact that he wasn't only a sheikh, wasn't only a surgeon, but was the Health Minister.

Why hadn't he told her?

She'd told him everything about herself—everything—and he hadn't even introduced himself properly. If he had, she would—would...

What would she have done? Not acted like a fool around him?

She doubted she could have done anything differently. He

only had to look at her, breathe near enough to fry her restraint circuits, unleash emotions and responses she hadn't known she'd come into this life equipped with and…

He should have told her!

But he hadn't. He'd kept her within those three feet throughout the very long workdays, as thoughtful, witty, infuriating, attentive, dominant, accommodating, provocative, appreciative, and just plain overwhelming as he'd been from that first moment. And to add insult to injury, he'd kept milking her for more intimate details about her life. And no matter how she tried to hold back something of herself, he just drew it out of her as if by magic, giving back nothing, until she felt she was standing naked in front of a two-way mirror where he sat in the dark on the other side, watching her unseen, unfathomable.

And here he was, striding towards her, his sight and presence overriding her logic and control. It made her mad. He made her vulnerable. And she couldn't let herself be. She had to put up resistance, wait it out. It would end all too soon.

"Janaan—you didn't get any sleep!"

Something alarming thrummed behind her sternum at the concern that hardened his voice, his gaze, made her step backwards when he would have taken her arm.

She covered her reaction in levity. "Look who's talking."

His gaze softened, conquering the scolding. "Let's not look. Shaving is a distant memory, and I've metamorphosed into a thug. No, wait—the thug phase was the first three days. I'm now in the pirate one."

Yeah. Right. And she wondered which phase was even more arrhythmia-inducing. "And look who's being ridiculous…"

She choked. She had no brakes where he was concerned.

He only laughed, that heart-breaking laugh of his. "That's my Janaan, the only one I count on to smack me over the head—even if it's with a compliment this time…" He scratched his beard in a cross between uncertainty and teasing. "I guess."

It was no use. Her lips spread on sheer pleasure that he was near, that he existed. "Don't guess. You accomplish Herculean tasks without blinking, but shaving is a big deal?"

"*Aih, ed'hukki*—laugh at a poor man's expense with your time-defying smoothness." He pantomimed running his fingers down said smoothness. She *felt* each touch, barely stopped herself from jerking away. "And to think women lament what they do to maintain their beauty. Try shaving twice a day."

"You mean you don't have someone or two to do it for you?"

He pouted. "What, alongside those assigned to scratching my itches? Wonder whatever befell them this past week."

She squeezed her eyes shut. "OK—that was stupid and prejudiced..."

"The 'never apologize' rule, remember?" His eyes held only amusement, soothing her. "And then I *can* have others waiting on my every whim. So you have a good excuse to think it."

No, she didn't. She knew how unfair that comment had been.

She knew he didn't abuse his privileges just as she knew he hadn't been bequeathed his position. In the past week she'd pieced together how he'd risen to it. How previous ministers had centralized medical care, squandered resources, imported protocols that hadn't worked for the culture and environment.

Then he had come, with a comprehensive vision of where Damhoor was and should go, with updated knowledge of medicine and the world and how to apply it here.

At thirty he'd been the land's leading surgeon, then he'd won his position, only to surpass its demands, rewrite its parameters. In the six years since he'd become Health Minister, he'd salvaged the medical system, reformed it, turned it into a model advanced countries were vying to emulate.

But she hadn't relied only on his people's reports in forming her opinion of him. Those could have been slanted by worshipping subordinates. She trusted the evidence of her eyes. The reports didn't do him justice.

"Even without bristles invading your face," he murmured, "you must be longing for the forgotten luxury of a bath." He advanced on her and she stumbled back. This time he noticed. His face lost all lightness, confusion draining his eyes of their usual bone-melting focus. "Anyway, we're returning to Halwan."

That made her find her voice again. "But only the rescue and medical relief work is done."

"That's what you signed up for. And you've gone above and beyond the call of duty. Rebuilding Mejbel is Damhoor's job, government and people. I set up a system with GAO that will keep the camp and field hospital running smoothly until everyone is back home or has a home built. The good news is I went over the hardest-hit areas at dawn and the water has almost receded. Some parts are coming back to life. Rebuilding can start soon."

"You went without me!"

"I couldn't bring myself to wake you up. You'd only been sleeping half an hour when the survey flight was scheduled."

"You mean when *you* scheduled the survey flight. When you haven't slept at all. Oh, Malek, I wanted to see that!"

"And you will, on our way out of here. After all you've done to help during the disaster, you must see its end."

"What about our patients?"

"All serious cases we've kept here to follow up will be airlifted to Halwan. You can follow up any of your personal patients any time." His voiced suddenly thickened. "I checked on Adham just half an hour ago. His coma is lightening."

He understood, shared her specific concern. He was incredible. He was also dead on his feet.

"I was coming to tell you that and to...er..." A spaced-out look came into his eyes. "*Azeff elaiki*—as we say here—bring you news of your imminent release in a—a festive procession..." He groaned. "OK, literal translation didn't work there. If it ever does..." He stopped again. "That's it—I'm officially delirious. I jumble Arabic and English only when all my synapses are fried. Good thing we're leaving in an hour." Before he turned away, he cocked an eyebrow at her. "And, Janaan, do check with Saeed about our departure. I may have hallucinated it all."

"You were born this way, weren't you?" Malek growled.

Jay refused to let his irritated vehemence intimidate her and held his infuriated gaze.

Something rumbled deep in his chest. "I bet you drove the doctor who delivered you crazy, dictating non-negotiable terms about the specifics of your delivery."

"What does my delivery have to do with you trying to deliver me to this seven-star hotel?" She waved a hand across her window at the Taj Mahal-like edifice. "I already have a room with all my stuff waiting for me in a hotel I can afford."

"If there were a championship for being perverse, you'd rake in every medal. *B'Ellahi*, why won't you let me do this for you?"

"Because I like the hotel room just fine, thank you. Because I'm not in the habit of accepting six-figure gifts, which a stay of even ten days in this hotel will amount to. And because you don't owe me anything, even if it seems you think you do. Besides, GAO will be providing my accomodations soon."

"You think I'm repaying you...?" He drove both hands into the depths of his luxurious hair, seemed about to pull it out. "*Ya muthab'bet al agl wad'deen!* And this is one occasion where literal translation works. I do need God to tether down my mind and faith with you around or they'll fly out the window."

"One sure way not to have me around is to drop me where I specified." She scowled back. "And for your information, I had no say in my delivery. I was born by Cesarean section."

"You see? You wouldn't get out, had to be forced out!"

"Like you're tempted to do to me now?"

"As if I could. I suspect the good doctor only got the best of you because your obstinacy was still in its infancy." His exhalation flayed her even from two feet away. "*Zain.* Fine. I will take you to your hotel. At least I get to do that at last. *But*—and this, Janaan, is something you won't win, so save your exasperation—I *am* taking care of the time the room was reserved while you were with me."

She wondered at the level his beauty attained with aggravation. Whoever had coined "beautiful when angry" didn't know the half of it. She shrugged. "*Zain* yourself. Sounds fair."

He looked flabbergasted. "What? No struggle? You're conceding? You're accepting, just like that?"

She couldn't help it. She giggled. "You said to save my exasperation."

"And that was the right phrasing for the tongue-holding, stubbornness-halting incantation? If only I'd known earlier." His lips spread, against his will it seemed, before that glazed look entered his eyes again. "You're lucky I'm operating on a flat battery." He lowered the barrier between them and his driver, muttered her hotel's address then sprawled beside her. "Excuse me as I recharge on the way. But if you don't wake me when we arrive, I'll..."

"Yes?" she prodded when he didn't come up with anything.

"*Ma ba'ref.* I don't know, something dire..." he promised as he slipped into sleep.

Jay waited a few moments then rested her head inches from his, absorbing his every detail with far more greed than she'd done as he'd slept on the helicopter.

This time *would* be the last time.

But though the knowledge hurt—and she couldn't dwell on how much it did—she was grateful for every minute she'd had with him. The past week, through the toil and exhaustion, working side by side with him to reach so many people in their acute need had been the best time of her life. But it was getting to know him that had catapulted it to the status of once in a lifetime. She counted herself lucky that she had met him, had been allowed to share that worthwhile time with him.

She suddenly remembered jeering at him the day they'd met, about his nights of excess, when he'd been returning from a three-week stint organizing the relief and relocation of Ashgoonian peasants whose villages had been destroyed in even worse torrential rain. That made it over a month he'd been literally on his feet, salvaging hundreds of thousands of lives.

And again she wondered that he'd let her get away with the slur. More than anything, she wondered why a man in his position would undertake such distressing, dangerous missions when he could just send people and resources.

But the answer was clear. He'd been born into ultimate privilege, wielded his power with the ease in which he breathed, but he thought nothing of dipping his hand in dirt and himself in pain and danger to fulfill the vocation he'd undertaken of his own choice, when any other man would have multiplied his wealth and power, when he'd only had to let his royal status secure him everything he wanted from life.

But it was clear what he wanted from life. The same thing she did. To be of use, to make a difference. But with his powers he was of infinite use, made such a far-reaching difference.

The car stopped. So did her heart.

God—it had only been fifteen minutes. Now she'd have to wake him to say goodbye. *Just get it over with.*

His name came out a choked whisper. "Malek."

He jerked up, his eyes snapping open on a blast of alarm and confusion. "Janaan. What…?" He subsided. "*Ya Ullah*—I had this dream…and you were… But you woke me up!"

"You told me to," she protested.

He blinked forcefully. "I'm still not sure if I'm dreaming this, if you didn't leave me sleeping to teach me a lesson."

"I said I would wake you up."

"You could have only let me believe it so I'd—"

She interrupted him. "If I give my word, I keep it. We arrived, I woke you up, and as much as I'd love to listen to you on the untrustworthiness of my gender, I have to say goodbye and let you—finally—get to your bed."

He bit his lower lip, his eyes steamy slits glowing in the limousine's semi-darkness. Then he sat up, got out of the car. She knew what he'd do, had to beat him to it. She opened her door and sprang out. There was no way she was prolonging this.

He caught her elbow when she tried to hurry away. "Seems the incantation has worn off. Do I need to re-invoke it?"

Just end this. "Malek, you're dead on your feet and I'm dying for that bath. So—let's just say our goodbyes here." She tried to regulate her breathing so she wouldn't gasp like a fish thrashing on the pavement. She also had to—*had to*—tell him. "But before I go, I want to tell you that the last week has been my life's most incredible experience. I'm grateful that you let me be a part of it all and—and that people like you exist."

She swayed, whimpered, tried to turn around. He lunged for her arm, his grip fierce as he turned her towards the entrance of her hotel. Her moaned objection was met by his groan, thick and ragged. "Not another word, Janaan. I'm taking you to your door."

It was a strange and not particularly pleasant experience, to be treated like some sort of celebrity in the two-and-a-half-pretending-to-be-four-star hotel where she'd previously had nothing more than inattention and grudging courtesy.

Everyone's first sighting of Malek had been dramatic, to put it mildly. Eyes had turned on her and it had been like watching one of those sci-fi movies where people switched identities in mid-stare. She had a feeling they'd provide their bodies in lieu of ground for her to walk on from now on.

Everybody made way for them so by the time they reached her door, the hotel felt deserted. He opened it for her, stood back.

She took the unsteady step that would take her out of his realm, crossed the threshold, turned to him, praying he'd just turn around and leave, spare her this.

He didn't. He stood looking down at her, tall and broad and indescribable, something poignant, defeated in every line of his body.

And she couldn't say goodbye. Not like this.

And it wasn't because she now knew what he was, because they'd shared that grueling experience or because she couldn't bear seeing fatigue shadowing his face and dimming the indomitable life force she'd been amazed by.

It was because depletion had bared a vulnerability she hadn't imagined. She sensed he needed solace, reprieve, and had never thought to ask for them, didn't think they existed.

She stepped back over the threshold, wrapped trembling arms around all she could of him.

He stiffened in her embrace as if she'd electrocuted him.

Oh, God. She'd read it all wrong. He didn't need comfort, not from her. He thought she was coming on to him!

Her feverish thoughts crashed and burned to ashes. All his tension was draining on a shuddering groan, his formidable body surrendering in her hold. He didn't hug her back, just let her hug him, and hug him, moaning, resting his head on hers, swaying with her to the erratic cadence of their heartbeats.

Then realization hit her. He was a man of state, in a conservative country. She was compromising him, hugging him in a hotel corridor that had to have prying eyes, no matter how deserted it felt to her oblivious senses.

Fear won over her greed to give him more solace, made her tear her arms off him. A rumbling moan of loss and reproach reverberated like distant thunder in his chest.

It made up her mind for her.

And she stammered, "Would you like to come in?"

CHAPTER EIGHT

MALEK FELT JANAAN'S words spearing through him, unraveling what her arms hadn't undone of his sanity.

He'd been feeling her withdrawing from him, had been steeling himself for the end that was advancing like a tidal wave of despondency. Then it had been the last seconds, the last glimpse, and she'd surged back into his existence, contained him in her arms, her haven. Then she'd made her offer.

He had no idea what it was exactly but, whatever it was, he couldn't take anything. Not when he wanted everything. Not when he had nothing to offer in return.

"Come in, Malek."

This time she wasn't giving him a choice but demanding he comply. He did, surrendered, let her take his hand and lead him inside. He could withstand almost anything, but he couldn't bear letting her fade out of his life.

But she was still there, drawing him deeper into hers, resolve and shyness in her eyes like at their first meeting. There was more now. Gentleness. Generosity. Solicitude.

Then a sudden burst of anxiety wiped away everything. She dropped his hand, swung away.

What had happened? What had gone wrong?

Now she'd ask him to get out. Or he'd wake up.

"I'm sorry, Malek. It's just—just…" She paused, her throat

working in agitation. "I've seen you do so much for others—and I wanted to—to do something for you—to show you, beyond words, how much I appreciate…" She paused again before blurting out, "But your…family must be waiting for you…"

So that was it. What so troubled her.

"You think I would have kissed you the first day we met if I had a…family?"

"You didn't…well, you almost, but you didn't."

"Oh, I did." He huffed a harsh laugh. "The almost was all the phone's fault. Now I let you hug me, came into your room. I'd have to be a dishonorable, unfaithful wretch if I did all that with a…family waiting for me. Is that what you think I am?"

"No." Her denial was ready, vehement. It validated him, made him proud. Her next words made him ashamed. "It's just I don't know...anything about you…"

And as long as he didn't tell her anything, he could delude himself he had a right to feel for her.

"You have nothing to worry about in that area," he rasped, feeling as if he was lying, heard his voice alien in his ears, thick with hunger, rough with agitation. He shouldn't be doing this. He could do nothing else. He had to have more of her. Just a little bit more. "So—what did you have in mind?"

Her heavenly eyes melted with that look that hurt him with its magnanimity, its uniqueness. "You look finished…"

He hadn't seen that coming. He barked a laugh. *"Shokrun."*

"You *know* what I mean! And *I* know you're a prime specimen of the exasperating species who accept help from no one."

"Takes one to know one, eh?"

She giggled. "Well, yeah. But I was hoping you'd let me…" She stopped, looked as if she was getting ready to jump off a cliff. Then she did. "Pamper you!"

He choked. She was out to give him a stroke today!

He staggered, leaned back on the door they'd just closed, coughed, felt the air disappearing, the world receding.

So this was temptation. Unstoppable, disempowering, to die for. This golden virago who'd invaded his life, occupied his being, conquered his reason and priorities.

She planted her hands on her hips, her eyes narrowing into slits of blue fire. "Are you laughing?"

He did laugh now, at the sheer inaccuracy of her suspicion. "No, but I may be dying."

"Ooh!" She stormed around, threw her bag on her bed, took off the jacket he'd given her, came back to him, thrust it at him. "I take it back. Now, take your jacket back and go laugh yourself to death somewhere else where you have access to emergency medical services. This emergency doctor isn't equipped for intubation and ventilation at the moment."

And he could only do one thing. Give up. All of himself, to her, to do with what she would. He only hoped he'd survive whatever she had in mind. He was already half-disintegrated from a hug and a statement of intent.

He blocked her path when she headed for the bathroom. She evaded him and he intercepted her again, spread his arms.

"Ana kol'ly elek." And he was, all hers.

She probably thought he meant he was all hers to pamper. A last flicker of sanity stopped him from elaborating.

After a hesitant moment, she beamed up at him, let out a carefree trill and dragged him behind her.

Once inside the bathroom she said, "Shower or shave first?"

"You're offering..."

"A shave. The shower you'll take on your own."

He grimaced in not-so-mock disappointment. "Spoilsport. But if I'm to prioritize, a shave has become an emergency by now."

"A shave it is." She ran out, returned with the dressing-table's chair, placed it in front of the mirror and patted it.

He sank on it, watched her hungrily as she strode out again and picked up the phone. She made three phone calls in all, her voice low. Preparing a surprise? Could he stand another one?

Two minutes later he heard a knock on the door. She came back from opening it triumphantly waving a zipped shaving kit.

She started lining up the products on the sink. "I decided to make use of your clout here, as it *is* for you after all."

He returned her smile, tried to convince his senses not to riot as her heat and softness pressed closer while she tucked his hair out of the way.

"About your shaving qualifications…"

She tossed her hair, looked down on him in mock disdain. "You'll have to trust me, sir. I'm a doctor."

He chuckled, surrendered to the soothing, distressing experience of having her capable fingers gliding over his face in the smoothness of foam, her intoxicating breath filling his lungs as she concentrated on details, her face inches from his.

He moaned a surplus of enjoyment and torment. "You know you're the first to ever shave me?"

Her eyebrows shot up. "Strange. Most men who aren't sheikhs with hordes of aides shave at some barbershop sometimes."

"My barber cuts my hair, period." He drove his hand through it, winced. "On the rare occasions I let him, that is."

She sighed. "Cutting hair like yours should be outlawed."

A laugh ripped from him. "You'd like to see it longer?"

Something blazed in her eyes—hunger? Longing? Before he could work it out, she snatched it out of reach, lowering her eyes, a playful smile hovering on her lips. "Mid-back would be nice. So, what have you got against being shaved?"

He brought the urge to grab her and rekindle that lost expression under precarious control, heard his voice thickening as he murmured, "Among other forms of being waited on, it's too... personal. I'm a bit of a fanatic about personal space."

Her hand froze after she'd shaved the first swathe down his beard, exposing his grateful skin. "If you're not comfortable… The whole point is to make you comfortable…"

He grabbed her hand as she moved it away, put it back to his face. "I am far, *far* beyond comfortable."

Her color deepened, then she gave a giggle and resumed. "So now you'll start hankering after getting shaved."

"Not if it's not you on the other end of the razor."

She met his gaze in the mirror, her lips deep red and moist, her eyes radiating azure intensity. Would they look like that, would she flay him with such focus and welcome as he rose above her, spread her, took her silken legs over his hips…

Ya Ullah. So there was such a thing as torture by arousal.

She tilted his head against her breast to gain access below his jaw. The moment her firmness cushioned him, he groaned with the surge of sensations, felt his grip on consciousness slipping.

He jerked to the feel of her hand gliding over his face. He blinked at his clean-shaven reflection. When had she done that?

"The good news is you don't snore," she teased.

He sat up, dazed. "It's getting alarming, these side trips to the twilight zone every time I sit still."

"Nothing a good night's sleep won't cure. But first—a shower. Go ahead as I put things in motion."

All he wanted to do was rise, press her to the door and devour her, then take her to bed and finish her. Still—to his total shock—*this* was as satisfying. He needed her gentleness and generosity as much as he did her passion, needed… Needed?

He'd never needed. He'd been born into so much, need had been non-existent. He'd filled its void with purpose, goals, action, achievement. But now, this—*this* was need.

And it was so unknown he had no way of fighting it. He was sinking in her care and compassion, no thought left in him of denying himself the pleasure and privilege of her.

She skipped out of the bathroom. "And no filling the tub. There's no way I'm budging you out of there if you fall asleep."

He followed orders, showered vigorously, trying to wake himself up. He had to savor each moment with her.

He came out feeling as if he'd regained his old skin, and she pointed out the clothes on the bed, said "Saeed" as she rushed past him to her turn in the bathroom.

So she'd called Saeed. He'd bet Saeed's speed in complying with her request had been for her, not him. During the past week Saeed had fallen under her spell, too.

Suddenly his blood roared in his ears, the lash of hormones an electric current jolting him to full wakefulness.

She was singing in the shower!

Elal Jaheem. To hell with duties and impossibilities. To hell with it all. He'd go in there, snatch her in his arms, let the water inundate them as it had the past week, this time warm, fusing, a medium for ferocity, for delirium. He'd knead and suckle her every inch, her every secret, deluge her in satisfaction, have her weeping for more, for him, and only then would he take her, then take her again…

At the bathroom door his storming steps faltered. He staggered the last one, leaned on the door, his ear to it, his hands miming caresses over her wet satin skin, listening to her emanating magic, feeling her influence tightening over his senses and will.

He knew she'd take him if he went in there. She'd open herself to him with all her fire and magnanimity.

And he couldn't do that to her. Not when he understood her need, of all people, for nurturing and being nurtured, for stability and continuity, for a total, unconditional, permanent alliance. Everything he could never give her. He'd be beyond dishonorable if he succumbed. He'd be cruel. Criminal.

He turned on his heel, headed for the bed, dressed quickly.

He should leave. He shouldn't have come in, shouldn't have let her expose herself to this. He *would* leave, leave her a note, or just go and call later. No, send Saeed with explanations—no, no explanations, just apologies, and a lifelong offer of any and every service and support he could provide…

"You're still awake!" He swung around at her soft exclamation, found her walking up to him, flushed, glowing, her hair a wet, darkened cascade over shoulders encased in a sleeveless stretch top echoing the color of her eyes, the rest of her curves cruelly hinted at in the layers of a flowing white skirt. She hurt him with her beauty. Then more when she ran a soothing hand down his back. "Must be the shower's rejuvenating effect. I feel like a new woman. At least the old one. How about you?"

He hadn't had time to take the coward's way out and now had to face her. He tried, began, "Janaan—"

"How about a massage while we wait for food? I evoked my carte blanche with Adnan. Ordered plenty of *logmet el guadi* so we won't have to fight over it."

"Janaan—I'm really tired—"

"Duh. I'm not asking you for a massage, I'm offering one." She took his hand in both of hers, guided him to the bed.

She pushed him down, tried to maneuver him face down, but he caught her to him, giving up again, knowing that he had to take this from her. But no more. Never more.

"Janaan, I don't want food, or more coddling, I just want to hold you. Let me hold you, *ya habibaty*."

She jerked at his intensity, at the endearment. He'd never said it to anyone before. He'd believed beyond a doubt he'd live his life never finding anyone to call his darling, his love. But he had. And she was. *She was.*

He tugged at her and she sagged in his embrace, shy, open, giving. He could take all she had, and she'd let him wring her dry. But he wouldn't—couldn't—take. He would never harm her…

But haven't you already? Aren't you harming her now?

Yes, he was. But for tonight the harm had already been done. And for tonight, he'd pretend there was a tomorrow, that this was the first night of the rest of their lives together.

He rose above her as she lay quivering beside him, her heat singeing him, her eyes luminous, ready and—*ya Ullah*—so trusting.

He turned her to her side, worshipped her in strokes that encompassed the perfection and uniqueness of her in wonder and frustration and regret. Then he wrapped himself around her and again felt he'd been created for just this purpose, this privilege, to shelter her, share with her.

"Malek." She moaned his name on a hot tremolo as she drove back against him, nestling into his body and being. And though he'd never felt such agony, with body and soul in the throes of a damaging arousal, she gave him something else he never thought to have. Peace. Profound and permeating.

He homed in on it, shutting out the uproar of voracity. Once it was all he felt, he plunged into it, sank…

The first thing Jay knew the moment she opened her eyes was that Malek was no longer around her.

She sat up in bed, her heart hammering, rattling her. Then she heard it. The shower.

He was still here.

She collapsed back with the reprieve. She'd have a little longer of him, even if it was only minutes…

The sun was trickling between the blackout curtains. They'd gone to bed at sunset, and she'd spent hours just feeling Malek all around her, absorbing his reality. She'd dreaded falling asleep and missing one breath, one heartbeat. But sleep had overcome her. She'd drowned in nightmares, in the agony of never getting the chance to say goodbye.

But he was still there. And she was no longer the same. The time of peace and intimacy in his arms had transfigured her.

This was the end, but he'd given her this. And it had been priceless, unrepeatable, something to power her through life.

The bathroom door opened and he stepped out, fresh, fully dressed and heart-wrenching. Longing and shyness almost stopped her heart as his heavy-lidded gaze raked disturbed, disturbing emotions over her. And she realized...

He didn't know how to say goodbye.

She just had to make it easier for him.

She rose to her feet, approached him when he stood there, staring at her. "*Sabah el khair ya* Malek. You look well rested."

His jaw clenched. "Janaan—we need to talk."

She groped for lightness, smiled. "That sounds ominous."

He clenched his fists, unclenched them. Then he spread his shoulders, stood straighter, almost formal. "Since your trip to Damhoor, and signing up with GAO were on the spur of the moment, you're unaware of many basic facts about the land. And about the specifics of the mission you've signed up for. I don't believe you know I am the mission's leader. I should have mentioned it."

Her heart did stop this time. Then it stumbled in a cacophony of shock and elation. This meant—this meant she'd have two whole months with him. *Sixty* more days!

She took a delighted step towards him. "Oh, Malek, that's *fantastic*! We'll be working together again..."

He took a step back, making her stumble to a halt. "No, we won't. I am not clearing you to join the mission."

CHAPTER NINE

MALEK WATCHED HIS words hitting Janaan like that flashflood had the disaster areas.

Seeing her eyes losing their animation, filling with incomprehension before the blow registered, was almost enough to make him retract them, forget all his resolutions. Almost.

"Why?"

He gritted his teeth against her pain, delivered the answer he'd been rehearsing since he'd woken up. "It's for the best."

She lowered her eyes, visibly struggling to keep the sudden tears that had filled them from falling. "I see."

Did she? He found himself struggling with the urge to rave and rant, trying to justify his decision, begging her to approve it, to exonerate him, to understand it was for *her* best.

"You don't want a woman like me on a mission you're leading. I know how men of your culture view easy women, and you no doubt think me that, think I'd be a liability."

That was what she saw? "Janaan…"

She raised eyes glittering with hurt and determination. "I admit it was only due to your restraint that nothing happened between us. But if you're afraid I think you've given me a green light to pursue you, that I'll make any sort of demand, you're gravely mistaken. I'm here to get to know the other side of my heritage while joining an effort I always wished to join.

Once it's over, I'll leave this country, where I'm clearly not welcome."

Malek would have been amazed at her resolve if he wasn't going crazy with fury at her conclusions.

She thought he believed her easy for offering him a night of unparalleled, unrepeatable solace? When he'd never known such contentment, such greed for more, for everything, with another human being? When he'd been blown away by her generosity, her guilelessness, her trust, by her fervent desire to lift his burdens and by how she truly had just by being near, even when he couldn't bring himself to share them with her? Though they hadn't made love, their night together had been his life's first true intimacy. He wanted more, would never stop wanting it.

And that was exactly why he had to send her away.

If she stayed within reach, he'd reach out for her. And she'd reach back. And she'd get hurt.

He was tempted to let her believe her version of the matter so she'd go. He couldn't. He owed her the truth. At least some semblance of it to explain why he was refusing her clearance.

"Janaan, every word you just uttered is pure insanity. There's no one like you. And I want you. I *want* you, Janaan. And that makes it unethical of me to include you on a mission where I'm not only your leader but your host and sponsor, too. It would be abusing my power, taking advantage of my position. Of you."

She gave a little laugh, a cornered, incredulous sound. "The concept of abusing your power doesn't even apply. You're not my employer. I'm a volunteer, if you haven't noticed. I'm here offering all I can offer of my own free will, for free."

She meant far more than her medical services. She was offering all of herself, was telling him it was a conscious decision on her part, with no expectations in return.

Temptation rose to unendurable levels. But he had to fight it. For her. He shook his head, determined not to let this go any further. "I am more sorry than I can ever express, Janaan."

"But, Malek..."

He struggled to shut out the desperation that seized her face, felt the last words he'd say to her gut him on their way out. "No, Janaan. This is final. *Samheeni ya habibaty*."

He surely wouldn't forgive himself.

With a ragged goodbye, and one last look, one that would have to last him a lifetime, he turned and left the only woman he'd ever craved. The woman he loved.

Yes, loved. *Ya Ruhmaan*, how he loved her. He'd never thought he *could* love. Now he knew he could, to unimaginable heights, to fathomless depths, with all he had in him, knew he'd never love again. For his heart had woken up only to love her. And to love her forever.

Jay kept missing the keycard slot. She swore, feeling tears of agitation rushing to her eyes.

She felt like one big bruise. She shouldn't wonder at that with all the ricocheting she'd done in the last couple of months. Not to mention since she'd met Malek. And that last blow before he'd walked out of her room that morning. And tomorrow she'd be veering off on another tangent, out of Damhoor. Never to return.

She pulled in a deep breath and tried to fit the card in her door again—and it receded out of reach!

Her eyes snapped up, a dozen unformed fears leaping in her mind, and there, in the semi-darkness, stood *Malek*.

Everything fell away. He was here. *Here*.

She couldn't think why. Couldn't think at all. Didn't care. He was here. He'd given her another chance to see him. She raised her face up to him like a sunflower would to the sun. And he was dragging her inside, his hands burning her with his reality and agitation?

"Malek?" she choked, dread mushrooming. Something had happened. Something personal this time.

"Don't even try to tell me you're not manipulating me this

time." Her mouth dropped open at his harshness. "And don't give me the 'I don't know what you're taking about' innocent routine. You know damned well what you did and why you did it."

She stared up at him, mute, uncomprehending.

His rage only spiked. "And you're not doing it. You are not going to Darfur, Janaan. I forbid you."

It took a moment for his meaning to sink in as his eyes and breath blasted her.

Answering anger snapped her out of her enervated state, made her shake off his hands. "You may be lord of all you survey where GAO missions in your region are concerned, but you have no say outside it." He smiled, ridiculing, arrogant, almost vicious. She cried out, "You can't have that kind of reach!"

One eyebrow rose, all malicious challenge. "Can't I?"

So he could. Now she knew.

"What about all this talk about not abusing your power?" she seethed.

"Oh, I'll make an exception this time."

This was a side to him she hadn't suspected. The ruthless sheikh who thought nothing of forcing people to bow down to his whims. It made her as mad as hell.

"How dare you?" she snarled. "You already deprived me of this mission, but how dare you presume to interfere in my decisions when they in no way impact on you?"

"I beg to differ." He seemed to expand, his voice taking on a frightening edge. And she wondered what he'd be like with all his refinement and restraint gone. He'd be a destructive force of devastating magnitude. "Missions in Darfur are dangerous. And you will not go where you'll be in danger. I forbid it."

Their gazes dueled for a long moment. Then she turned away, processing what he'd said, elation over his concern for her well-being seeping into her soul, warming it after the deep-freeze where seeing the last of him had plunged it.

It didn't warm it enough to melt her anger. She turned on him again. "Thanks for the concern, but I've fended for myself all my life and I *won't* let you dictate my actions. Darfur was always my second choice, and I always knew that joining GAO carried risks. I'm not less than the other volunteers who risk their lives daily. At least I have no one who needs me or will be hurt if something happens to me."

Malek felt her words hacking at him like razors.

That she'd go where she'd be in danger, where he couldn't reach her, tampered with his sanity. That she expected something *would* happen to her during her service, that she accepted that it wouldn't matter—it was beyond endurance.

He roared, "You're only doing this to force me to change my mind, forcing me to choose the lesser evil!"

A disbelieving, sarcastic sound crackled on her lips. "How could I have been sure you'd find out about my plans before I left tomorrow for them to have the desired effect? And why should I think endangering myself would sway you when I thought your reasons for refusing my assignment had nothing to do with me and everything to do with preserving your honor and your position?"

Would his head burst in outrage? "You think this self-preserving, unfeeling...*rot* motivated my decision?"

"I think myself too insignificant to have done so."

And at that moment he was capable of fatal violence. Too bad the bastard who'd damaged her most was already dead.

He finally snarled, "You're a fool, Janaan, to even think anything so unfounded of yourself. Is that what your father and those siblings made you believe? *They're* insignificant. You can't let their selfish cowardliness affect your self-worth."

She gave an easy shrug. "I *don't* think I'm insignificant to the world at large, just to someone of your status, someone who has to look at the bigger picture. Contrary to thinking you self-preserving or unfeeling, I've seen how selfless and compassionate you are..." She stopped, glared at him. "Or, at least, can be." She walked to the door, opened it for him. "Now, if you'll, please, leave so I can get ready for my early flight?"

He took the door from her, closed it with great restraint. "You're going nowhere but under my protection. Whatever your reasons for signing up for Darfur, they worked."

She gave him a withering look. "That's presuming I still want to join *your* mission. Which I don't. I'm not going where my presence is considered the lesser of two horrors, where I'm considered a liability. I accept the blame for this label as I indulged in an inappropriate level of intimacy with you, but I can't do anything about it now but promise that you'll never see me again."

He grasped her shoulders when she made to turn away. "I take *all* the responsibility for whatever happened between us. And you wanted to join this mission, *wa b'Ellahi'l allei'l Uzeem*, you're joining it even if I have to haul you there and keep you under lock and key."

He let her go as if her flesh burned him, stalked to the door.

Before he closed it behind him he rasped over his shoulder, "And, Janaan, don't worry. The three-feet rule is over. During the coming two months, I promise to keep my distance."

CHAPTER TEN

MALEK KEPT HIS promise. For two weeks so far. They'd felt like two bleak—if madly busy—years.

Jay didn't know what she would have done without Hessuh and Saeed's companionship. They'd made it possible to bear Malek's alienation, and had also become her guides to the ways of the land and communicating with its people.

They'd embarked on their mission the very next day in a convoy of a mobile surgery unit, ob/gyn, dentistry, internal medicine and ophthalmology units, twenty accommodation trailers, six Jeeps and two ambulances. It was mind-boggling the resources Malek had made available to GAO.

They'd reciprocated by sending thirty volunteers, including her. And knowing that Malek couldn't spare enough medical staff post-disaster, in addition to the logisticians, health educators and cultural experts who made GAO rise above other humanitarian efforts, a good percentage of the thirty were doctors. She was the only emergency doctor. Malek was the only surgeon.

He had brought along the same number, including his aides and core team from the relief efforts. As far as humanitarian missions other than in time of disaster went, this one was a whopper.

They'd traveled south through Damhoor, bypassed all reasonably self-sufficient towns and villages, made their stops at communities of semi-settled *Badu* in their winter camping grounds along the borders.

The third tribe they were with, Bani Hajjar, was like the other two before it, leading their lives according to customs that hadn't changed in millennia. But while that was efficient for the most part, it hadn't done their health much good.

In the desert you survived if you were born robust and stayed that way. Acute illnesses and injuries were usually fatal, and chronic diseases that modern medicine had long since found cures for or controlled were treated with tribal remedies, but it was accepted that the afflicted would be *aleel*, sickly, and remain so until they withered and died.

They still had a major job of convincing the tribe to accept what modern medicine had to offer them. When they succumbed, she felt it was only due to their awe of Malek.

He organized both teams' efforts, gave her the leader's position within GAO's medical team. When she wasn't fulfilling the demands of her position, she was sharing the ob/gyn unit with Hessuh, her trailer-mate, and together they'd taken care of hundreds of women, in an incredible variation of conditions. More incredible was what these women put up with health-wise, and still functioned well, practically supporting the whole tribe's way of life.

Although they were less segregated than town and village women, and weren't generally veiled, they had a much lower status than men but certainly worked the hardest. Tending flocks, doing housework, cooking, raising children, drawing water, spinning and weaving, setting up and dismantling tents. She'd invariably overestimated a woman's age by ten to fifteen years. It was accepted here that a woman would be worn out and old by forty.

With each case Jay felt her blood boil at their conditions and, worse, their acceptance of them.

Hessuh had just finished examining a woman who, after looking her and Jay over, had launched into a defense of their way of life, extolling how women were protected by a strict code of honor, could move about relatively freely and were allowed to sing and dye their long hair with henna.

"Protected, strict code, *relatively* freely—*allowed*!" Jay mumbled as soon as the woman stepped out.

Hessuh gave her a placating pat. "It's too entrenched. They know nothing else, think there's nothing else to know, or should be known. So don't you start preaching women's lib."

"You're saying they should be left as they are?"

"I'm saying it's sometimes not right to import our views of what's right or fair," Hessuh said, making Jay feel like an overzealous fool. Her next words defused the feeling—on purpose, Jay bet. Hessuh was an astute, thoughtful woman. "And then time and the march of civilization work wonders. This woman was my grandmother. Look how far I've come since her generation."

"If you're the example of what waiting for natural progression to install changes brings, I'm all for it," Jay said. "You're one amazing woman, Hessuh."

Hessuh laughed. "The way you speak your heart and mind, whether it's good or bad, never ceases to amaze me, Jay. We're not big on that here and it's *aib*...shameful to express what you *genuinely* feel or think. Another reason it's such a pleasure to be around you is that you don't make digs at me."

"Who can make digs at you? You're great, all around."

Hessuh smirked. "Other women, of course. Feminine jealousy is elevated to an art here, so it's something to bear in mind when you're judging women's conditions. Some of women's worst and most vocal enemies here are women. I am unmarried, so a danger to every woman's husband, especially as I'm also loose and naked." She looked wryly down her modestly attired, lithe, curvaceous body. "I'm a doctor so I make them feel underachieving and so on. But instead of wishing or trying to change their status, they attack mine."

"A case of the oppressed becoming the oppressor, huh?" Jay

chewed her lip thoughtfully. "I guess every victim has some responsibility in perpetuating their suffering."

Hessuh sighed. "Apart from the social ranks at the top, it is women who single-handedly raise children here. It's they who raise their male children to think of women as lesser beings."

"Why?"

"As I said, patriarchal conditioning has become a part of the female psyche here. And then there is another feminine side to the equation. A man here brings his wife to the family home. A mother wants to make sure her son will bring her a subordinate as she'd been to her own mother-in-law."

"But—that's sick!" Jay cried.

"It's how it works. But as I said, time is changing things. My sister is married to a Damhoorian engineer who thinks her more than his equal. So it's not all doom and gloom. The less advantaged classes are where social rigidity and injustices are most perpetuated, not only here but all over the world."

Jay gave a slow nod. "I guess you're right. Wow, Hess. You keep giving me insights into the culture I would have never come to see on my own. Getting to know *you* is one of the best ways I'm learning about Damhoor today."

Hessuh's lips twisted. "You mean an unmarried woman in her early thirties in a land where marriage is viewed as a woman's only reason for existence and where a woman over twenty-five is an *ajooz*, a hag? An obstetrician when marriage is considered a woman's only viable 'career'?"

"Yeah, all that. Also unveiled when all the local women I've seen wear veils to one degree or another. How come?"

"That's another example of what time and the right people in the right places can achieve." Hessuh smoothed the gleaming wealth of her long mahogany ponytail. "I personally owe being unveiled to Sheikh Malek. He made a decree that women who work in the medical field can dress however they choose—but only a handful took him up on his offer. He also lets girls enter medical school here when our only local female doctors had their education abroad, like I did, also thanks to the vision of another man—my father. In the last six years the number of females in medical school has risen to almost that of the males."

So it had come back to Malek again. As it always would.

Hearing about him and his achievements, which was constant when everyone, even her GAO partners, had something new to relate about him, only slashed at her rawness.

She groped desperately for a change of subject. "So, to continue my curiosity—what does Hessuh mean?"

"Share," Hessuh said briefly, a challenging expression on her face, as if she was daring Jay to make a comment.

Jay obliged. "So that's why you *share* everything with me!"

Hessuh let out that ready, tinkling laugh. "I knew you couldn't resist it. My name is the noun, not the verb, dear lady. Though don't ask me what my father was thinking when he named me. Share of what, *b'Ellahi*? I always asked him. After thirty years of racking his brains, he came up with a satisfying answer. I'm his share of life's happiness."

"And you're my share of this mission's," Jay teased. "I wouldn't replace you with the lion's share."

Their banter was interrupted by their next patient, a woman of sixty who Jay mistook for almost eighty, with a jarring pink and violet dress and blue dots tattooed all over her face.

After careful examination they looked at each other and nodded. This woman was there to check them out, no more. As Jay punched in her data on the computer, the woman insisted on enlightening them that electricity was trapped *jinn* whom God had enslaved in the wires to serve humans.

As the woman left, Jay stared after her open-mouthed.

Hessuh burst out laughing. "Wait until we go back to Halwan where your patients will make stock-market transactions from their cellphone internet connections while waiting for their CT session, then tell you you made them late for their *hegamah* and *roggiah* sessions. The first is the so-called cure-all by leeches and bloodletting and the second is the *jinn*-powered method of warding off the evil eye and extracting malevolent influences."

Hessuh laughed again as that expression took over Jay's face on just imagining the incongruities. "I should have my camera ready at all times. Your reactions are delightful."

"You're making me sound like a clueless tourist here!"

"Well…" Hessuh spluttered at Jay's mock indignation. "Oh, you're just a newcomer. Your wonder is very...refreshing."

Jay poked her. "That was 'laughable', wasn't it?"

Hessuh giggled again. Jay couldn't remember when she'd made friends with another person more easily or quickly. Except for Malek…

Malek. How she missed him, ached, *burned* for him.

God. Everything came back to him. Every thought, every hearbeat, every impulse streaking through her nerves.

It was far worse to see him and suffer his distance and formality after she'd basked in his nearness and spontaneity than not seeing him at all again.

All she could do now was count down the remaining weeks, pray she'd toughened up enough by now that they wouldn't hurt as much.

Oh, who was she kidding?

"*Doctorah* Janaan, we have an emergency!"

Saeed! Janaan jerked out of her torment, swung around.

"Here, or are we responding to a distress call?" she gasped.

"A distress call. A cave-in in a quarry around forty miles away." He rushed to carry her suitcase-sized emergency bag then rushed out after her, giving her that penetrating look that read her down to her last secret. He knew how she felt about Malek, probably even pitied her for the hopelessness of it all.

"Did you alert Ma—er, Sheikh Malek?" Jay asked, remembering that no one called him Doctor, that his sheikhdom superseded his medical status, and that here people called each other by their first name, not their family name, even in formal situations.

"Yes, he said to get you, ask you to organize an appropriate team. He's organizing the rescue operation."

And there he was. Malek. Taking charge of the surgery unit. Would he let her work with him again? Would he even look at her?

Get a grip, you pathetic fool. See to your job.

Angry, crushed by longing, humiliated by it, she rushed about, gathering the team best equipped for the emergency.

She jogged to the ambulance as Hessuh caught up with her. Steve and Elaine, her GAO nurses, followed, while one of Malek's aides took the wheel. Two more GAO nurses as well as Malek's Lobna and Alyaa went to the other ambulance, with Saeed driving. Then she realized they'd be following a camel-riding messenger!

"That's a racing camel," Hessuh said, reading her alarm. "He can do 40 miles an hour, easily keep up 25 miles an hour for an hour. On this terrain, we won't be able to top that speed ourselves."

Jay exhaled. "I hope the rescue choppers arrive before us."

Hessuh sighed. "Sheikh Malek says the quarry is uncharted and only this guy knows the way. Sheikh Malek will relay its position once we arrive—in less than two hours, hopefully."

Jay felt her stomach knotting. Less than two hours when every minute might mean someone losing their chance to be saved.

She could do nothing but sit and watch their guide prodding his galloping camel, and watch as the endless desert sped by.

She had a feeling this was very much what her life would be like from now on.

An endless desert speeding by.

CHAPTER ELEVEN

MALEK READ THE co-ordinates on his GPS as soon as the quarry came into sight and barked them in his cellphone to the rescue helicopters.

He brought his trailer to a halt as close as he could get and jumped out, his eyes taking in the scene.

A two-hundred-foot-high rock-cutting, gravel-extracting quarry hewn out of Aj-Jalameed mountain, now almost unrecognizable after the the massive avalanche.

Just imagining the effect it had had on flesh and blood, that there were people below that rubble, dead or dying or even only injured, in pain, trapped in horror for the long hours it had taken to alert them and bring them here. His blood boiled.

He hadn't known this quarry existed. And neither had any officials. This was an unsanctioned project, erected with no safety protocols. Those responsible for this exploitation of workers and resources would answer to him in person. But that would come later. He had to save their victims first.

And for that he needed Janaan with him.

He swung around to the two ambulances that had stopped behind him, found her jumping down from one, followed by the other personnel, rushing towards the scene. Not towards him.

And why would that wrench out his heart?

He'd told her he'd keep his distance, his implication that she must do the same loud and clear. And—*ya Rahmaan ya Raheem*—she'd done worse than that. She'd vanished. Only the evidence of the incredible job she was doing told him that she was still around.

He spent his days going insane, her scent filling his lungs, her voice ringing in his ears, her eyes and smile emblazoned on his retinas. He saw her everywhere, only to find her nowhere. Nowhere but on his mind, indelibly engraved. Then had come the nights. Soaked in delirium, his body convulsing with need, his heart corroding with hunger for one smile, one twinkle of her precious eyes.

He missed her with every breath. He missed her every breath. Nothing, not even preoccupation or exhaustion, lifted the longing, the gnawing. And she was there, within reach, and he couldn't reach out and take all the joy and ecstasy her essence and passion could bring him…

You're not important, ya moghaffal. *Get to your casualties.*

He ran after her towards the casualties who were strewn on the ground like broken toys. Gaunt men, working in inhumane conditions, for a pittance no doubt, now covered in rock powder, as if they'd been exhumed from their graves.

Could they be Damhoorians? Were any of his people in such a depth of need they'd debase and endanger themselves to that extent for crumbs? Or were they Ashgoonians? Or maybe Nussoorans?

He'd get to the bottom of this. And he'd put an end to it. But first those men.

Janaan and her team were already all around them, emergency bags open, supplies lined up and gurneys ready to transfer the most badly injured to the ambulances or to OR.

Saeed caught up with him, a dusty, scared man stumbling in his wake. "That's the foreman. He says his men pulled out those twelve with their bare hands. Two are dead. Twenty-four remain buried."

Before Malek could ask the first thing that burst into his mind, Janaan asked it. "Those men—how long were they buried?"

Saeed translated her question to the foreman. The man stammered out the answer. From one to three hours.

"And how long ago were they rescued?" she pressed.

The answer was the same.

She reached the same conclusion he did, announced it to her team. "We have to assume they developed crush syndrome." At the hesitant looks from those whose specialties had nothing to do with trauma, she elaborated, "After being crushed for more than an hour, on being released, crush syndrome develops, resulting in severe hypotension, renal failure and irreversible shock."

"So they might have only managed to kill them by pulling them out?" Steve Mittman asked. Malek didn't like the way the big, blond man was looking at Janaan. Didn't like it at all.

Janaan nodded. "Rescuing people from underneath rubble, without initiating aggressive fluid replacement during or right after the rescue, is termed 'rescue death'."

"At least we'll be right here when the rest are being pulled out." That was Hessuh, his pride and joy, prototype of the new breed of female Damhoorian doctors. She'd gotten so close to Janaan, gotten to share her trailer, breathe the same air. He envied her so much, he couldn't bear looking at her.

And there was Janaan, exchanging that look of unspoken understanding and camaraderie with her, not with him!

"For now, regardless of other injuries," Janaan said, "some may be beyond reach if the six-hour window when the syndrome becomes irreversible has passed. So here's the treatment plan." She rose to her feet, still not looking at him. "Pick a patient, then bilateral peripheral lines, glucose-saline, two liters over the next hour, two more over the next two, twelve in all today. Then airway management, ventilation and examination."

Then she fell to her knees between two of the casualties.

She behaved as if he wasn't there. Was she abiding by his order, or was she punishing him for it?

No—that would be manipulation and by now he was sure she didn't have a manipulative cell in her body. Maybe she knew they could deal with this, that his expertise would come later…

"Let me help."

Steve. With his boyish good looks and hot eyes. Advancing on Janaan, offering assistance, declaring interest. Hunger.

Janaan looked up, gave a tiny smile. A *smile*. Of acceptance, encouragement…? *W'Ullahi ma beyseer*!

By God, he wouldn't let it be. He fell to his knees by her side, growled up at Steve, "If you don't have a patient, help in the rescue efforts. The helicopters will be here any minute."

He dismissed Steve from his focus, turned his eyes on Janaan. Her face was still averted, scrunched up in…was it concentration? She cut off her patient's sleeves then reached for IV giving sets. He closed his hand over hers, taking one from her hand.

Her gasp blasted through him like a hot desert gale, her soft, capable hand going limp in his and letting both sets fall.

Still keeping her eyes off him, she withdrew her hand, turned to the others. "Elaine, Alyaa, Miguel, place catheters, then monitor urine output and pH. If it's dark brown or red then it has myoglobin. To flush it out to keep the kidneys working, we need to achieve a diuresis of at least 300 millilitres per hour with a urine pH of more than 6.5."

They nodded, got to it at once. They clearly considered Janaan their triage officer, even in Malek's presence. Janaan had really won his team's unswerving respect and obedience during the past two weeks.

And how couldn't she? Her knowledge was extensive, her work ethic impeccable, her people skills inimitable. Everyone recognized that and was giving each talent and asset its due.

He felt her eyes darting to him now, or rather to his hands, felt their gaze along his every nerve ending as she took in that he'd already started fluid replacement on one patient.

He looked up at her, needing that gaze to mesh with his, needing the connection. She didn't look back, turned to the other patient. He gritted his teeth, kept on working.

Ten minutes later, resuscitation was over and everyone reported the condition of their casualties. Then the helicopters were there and Janaan rushed after Malek to organize the airlift.

He directed his men's efforts while she directed their medical team in resuscitation before extrication.

It took over three hours of grueling work, and not a few accidents, the worst resulting in one of his men fracturing his femur, to get everyone out and resuscitated.

With triage sorted out, they loaded casualties on gurneys in preparation for transferring them to the ambulances or OR. Rafeeq went to ready the anesthesia station.

Janaan stood there taking stock. He approached her, needing some contact, some response. She still refused it.

Suddenly she asked, "Who will you start with?"

He didn't answer right away. Not because he hadn't made a decision but because he needed to bring the debilitating spurt of joy and relief at her acknowledgement of him again under control.

"This man." He pointed to the moaning man on the second gurney from where she stood. "His crush injury is the worst."

Her nod told him she thought so too. So had she only been making sure his judgment was the same as hers? Or had she been trying to initiate conversation?

No. Janaan didn't resort to things like that. That had been a legitimate question. To which he hadn't given a complete answer.

He had to add, "I may have to amputate." At her gasp, he rushed on, "I won't know until we have him on the table. But I just need you to be ready for the possibility."

She nodded, her color at high level. And he couldn't deny his need. He needed her with him.

"Will you assist me?" he rasped.

Her eyes swung up to him, letting him in again, blazing her relief to be included, her eagerness to be of help. To be with him again?

"Hada abbi."

Both Malek and Janaan jerked around at the adolescent voice, found a boy of no more than thirteen standing two feet away from them, covered in the yellowish dust, as if he too had been pulled from the rubble, undernourished, underdeveloped, swaying.

Malek took a stride towards him, his hand held out to support him, and the boy hiccuped a sob and stumbled back.

"Aish beeh? Aish rah t'sa'woh b'abbi?"

Malek closed the gap, took the boy by the shoulders, gently, carefully, talked to him, low and soothing. And the boy's sobbing escalated into all-out weeping.

"Malek?"

Janaan's trembling whisper touched him before her hand did. He first called Saeed, gave him orders, turned the boy over to him then turned to Janaan.

"This man is Aabed, Nabeel's father. Nabeel told me he was standing next to him when the cave-in happened. He pushed him away at the last moment. Nabeel has six younger brothers and sisters and he said he's too young to be the man of the family."

That vast compassion flared in her face, burned him. "What did you tell him? What did you tell Saeed to do?"

"I told him he has nothing to fear. I told Saeed to take care of him. Now we'll take care of his father."

"Is he under yet, Rafeeq?" Malek asked.

Rafeeq adjusted his anesthetic/oxygen delivery then raised his eyes. "Go ahead."

"Administer cephalosporin, please, Rafeeq." Malek raised his head at the moment's silence that greeted his order. "Yes, now, and tetanus toxoid. Infection with the state of circulation in his leg is taking root as we speak. We can't be too aggressive or too early in treating it."

He returned his eyes to the field of surgery, Aabed's left leg. It was blue, cold and pulseless. Not to mention grossly swollen up to the groin.

Jay eyes followed Malek's, the only thing she could see of him now, and shivered at the terrible intensity that prowled in their depths, like a caged lion pondering a way out.

She couldn't bear it. "What will it be, Malek?"

Malek was silent for a moment more. Then he exhaled. "I'll start with a fasciotomy. If we don't get definite distal pulses at the end of the procedure…"

He'd have to amputate. Then Aabed would lose his ability to stand on his own two feet, his only means of supporting his family. And Nabeel would lose his childhood to the struggle of keeping his family from starvation.

"He won't."

Her heart fired at Malek's whisper. Had she muttered her fears out loud?

As Malek held her gaze, she knew he only shared her thoughts, was reaching out with the promise. Nabeel, like Adham, would get the best chance at life. He'd make sure of it.

Then he moved his eyes back to his task, made a transverse incision across the thigh, dissected the subcutaneous tissue to expose the iliotibial band, made a straight incision through it in line with its fibers. She carefully reflected the fascia for him, exposing the intermuscular septum, watching the poetry in his every move, the genius and healing flowing from his fingers.

"Cautery, please, Janaan."

His baritone sent its gentleness through her on an almost uncontainable wave of longing. She clamped down on the tremors, coagulated all vessels in the now pale, spongy muscles. She withdrew, fell back into the reality of his nearness, the feeling that he seemed to be seeking her again, still afraid to believe it, expecting it to end at any moment.

She watched his every move as he made a two-centimeter incision in the fibrous septum, releasing the building pressure in the muscle compartments of the thigh which were now cutting off circulation and causing the starting necrosis of the whole limb.

"Metzenbaum scissors, please, Janaan." It was in his hand as he uttered its name. He used it to extend the incision. "OK. Anterior and posterior compartments released. Please measure pressure of the medial compartment."

She did, bit her lip. "Elevated," she rasped.

He inhaled, nodded, made another incision to release the adductor compartment. After two minutes he said, "And now?"

She measured again, felt her heart boom at the reading.

"Pressure within normal limits," she gasped.

He let out a long exhalation. Relief made audible.

"Your turn," he murmured.

She jumped in, making sure she didn't leave one bleeding artery uncauterized.

"That's perfect, Janaan. Now feel for distal pulses."

She felt for the pulse in Aabed's foot as Malek felt for the femoral and popliteal, bracing herself. A flutter tickled her fingertips. She moaned. "Oh, God…"

He came around her, felt where she had then dragged off his mask. "Pack the wound open, Janaan, and apply a bulky dressing."

"You mean…"

He turned heavy, full eyes on her. "Yes. This is a supreme case of *guddur w'luttuf*. God decreed adversity but was merciful with it." He turned his eyes to Aabed's leg and her eyes gushed with their loss, with fear he'd resume his distance, her deprivation. She blinked tears away, got to work.

"He'll be returned to OR for debridement until no necrotic tissue is left before we close the wound. But I believe he'll walk again." He looked at Rafeeq. "Great job, Rafeeq. Bring him round. Take him to IC then prepare for the next procedure."

Management and surgeries continued non-stop for the next fifteen hours. Four patients were beyond help, five were still critical, but the remaining would survive with minor or no handicap. All would have died without intervention. Saving twenty-five should have felt good. It didn't.

Malek had remained within those three feet of her, his eyes on her every second he didn't have them on his job, seething with so much that distressed her, that she couldn't fathom.

It was noon by the time they returned to their convoy. Their team was exhausted, physically and spiritually, as they made their way to their trailers. Malek walked her in silence to hers, seemed about to say something when Hessuh caught up with them and climbed inside before Jay.

After a long moment of hesitation, he only rasped, "Get some rest." Then he turned away.

She stumbled inside, found Hessuh in bed, fully clothed, eyes closed. Jay fell face down on her own bed, the last flicker in her receding mind an image of Malek as he'd left her.

Janaan moaned and burrowed into a wonderful feeling.

Hot, male, encompassing. *Malek.*

Only he made her feel this protected and cherished. This hungry, this incredible, and this miserable!

She opened her eyes, expecting the echoes of their night together to dissipate, leaving her cold and empty and alone—alone forever… And he was there. Then he didn't vanish.

Malek. He was really there. Stretched out beside her. Like that night in her hotel, drenching her in caresses. Disoriented, she blinked, at him, around the trailer.

"I asked Hessuh to leave us alone," he answered her unspoken question, the richness of his voice twisting in her heart, in her loins, the spike of sensation so severe her teeth rattled with its force. The drugged tinge to his gaze suddenly lifted, a dull bleakness replacing it. Then he was leaving her!

He staggered up to his feet, seemed to sway before he stood up straight. Or maybe it was her world that was churning, would never right itself again.

"*Habibati, samheeni*—forgive me, I saw you sleeping and I couldn't—couldn't... *Ya Ullah-hada w'Ullahi tholm.*"

Tholm. Injustice.

What was? That he was, that he made her feel all this?

She shakily swung trembling legs over the side of her bed, sat staring up at him with her hands helpless and cold in her lap, sick electricity flooding her body as he drove his hands in his hair like a man about to lose his mind.

Oh, God—was something wrong with him?

Then he suddenly growled, the sound of a man at the end of his tether, "My name is Malek ben Muraad ben Amjad ben Munsoor Aal Hamdaan."

She stared at him. Why was he telling her his...? Oh...

Oh God.

No. *No.* He couldn't mean...

From a long distance she heard a wavering rasp.

"*Muraad ben*... He's—he's..." She stopped, stared at Malek.

"Damhoor's king, yes. My father."

CHAPTER TWELVE

*D*AMHOOR'S KING. *Damhoor's* king. *Yes.* My *father. My* father.

The words ricocheted inside Jay's skull, building up to a cacophony that almost burst it apart.

It was all just too—too…

And she suddenly howled with laughter, hysterical, agonizing, bone-rattling laughter.

She laughed until her lungs shut down, until her eyes were wrung dry, until her insides twisted together in a knotted mess.

He watched her all through it, his eyes heavy, grim.

At long last the first enormity of shock and realization abated. It left her trembling, limp.

She finally rasped, "And to think you called *me* Janaan of the ceaseless surprises. First you're a sheikh, then a surgeon, then the Health Minister. Now you're a prince."

He made a frightening sound in his throat. Then he almost spat out, "I'm not *a* prince. I'm *the* prince. The crown prince."

Silence crashed down again.

Numb now, Jay finally gave a short, stunned giggle. "It just keeps getting better, doesn't it?" Then a distant memory struck her like a lightning bolt. "But...over a year ago, when my father started saying he'd get me a job here, get my mother a home, I researched Damhoor, and the crown prince's name was—was…"

"Majd," he muttered. "The *Glory* of Aal Hamdaan, as he truly was. My elder brother. He died of a ruptured brain aneurysm ten months ago."

His loss. This was it. The loss behind the hot empathy that had permeated her when she'd related her loss of her mother the day they'd first met, seemingly many lifetimes ago.

He suddenly closed his eyes, inhaled. He opened them a moment later, but she'd seen it. The spasm of anguish that had contorted his very being.

"We were just walking out of a squash court after a grueling match where he'd trounced me. And he just collapsed at my feet. I forgot everything, seeing him there—there was not a single medical shred left in my mind. For a whole minute. Then it was a blur of trying to keep him alive till I got him to the OR. He died before I got him into an ambulance."

She kept watching him, breathless.

He inhaled another breath. "I ordered the autopsy, attended it. My father begged me not to do it. I disregarded him. I knew a massive subarachnoid hemorrhage was the cause of death, but I had to ascertain exactly how and why—that there was no suspicion of foul play. I think it hit my father harder that I cut Majd open than that he'd died. He grew old and infirm in front of my eyes those hellish days. Then he accused me of causing Majd's death."

She surged up, shaking with horror, her hand begging permission to approach, to defuse the shock waves of his revisited anguish. He caught it, buried his face there, nuzzling her clammy flesh with the fierceness of a tiger seeking solace, the blackness of his voice, his pain, lancing through her.

"Majd was far frailer than I am, always pushed himself to fill his big-brother role."

"Aneurysms don't rupture on exertion and you know it!" Her vehemence was instant, final.

His let go of her hand, let his fall to his side, his lips twisting in self-revulsion. "If I didn't tire him to death, I caused his death in a different way. I'm the doctor in the family. Ever since I became one the whole family has let me take care of their health, make their every medical decision. Majd was not only the brother I worshipped, he was this land's crown prince. I should have checked up on him routinely. A simple CT or MRI to the brain would have detected the aneurysm in time to do something about it. He trusted me, and he died because of my negligence. I failed him."

This was what he lived with?

She caught his hand and squeezed it. She had to stop him doing this to himself. "You can't even let yourself think that. Since when are CTs and MRIs routine or done without serious indications? If he didn't have symptoms to warrant them, you know it's contraindicated to have them! There was no negligence on your part. You didn't fail him. It was fate."

His pupils dilated, like a black hole consuming the sun. She squeezed his hand harder, desperate to yank him out of his mire of guilt and self-hatred. He resisted her for a moment. Then he succumbed, snatched her hand to his lips, his eyes burning with gratitude, acknowledging her intentions, if not their validity.

She'd thought his name so fit him, lord and owner of her heart, king of all men in her eyes. How little she had known.

And though she'd never thought he'd ever be within reach again, it was only now that she felt him...vanish. Forever. She withdrew her hand, let it fall, a useless, lifeless thing by her side.

It didn't seem he noticed her withdrawal, pressed closer, intent on sharing the rest of his torment, unable to stop now he'd started. "As a younger son, the odds were that the throne would never fall to me and I was left free to pursue my goals. Then the unthinkable happened and I'm no longer free. This mission is my last indulgence in my old life, my old purpose, before I'm forced to relinquish my vocation to take on the mantle of diplomacy in preparation for the time when I'm forced to ascend to the throne. But that isn't why..."

His words halted, something imploring entering his eyes. She heard the rest loud and clear.

This isn't why I tried to push you away.

She felt a strange detachment descend on her as she watched him struggle with revealing just why, her mind a blank.

"Majd had two daughters, so now I, next in line to the throne, must choose a possible future queen from the list of acceptable women from our major tribes. I must choose a bride to produce an heir. At the time the succession fell to me, I considered it just another duty I'd have to fulfill. But now, though this won't happen a minute before I'm forced to, months—*years* if I can at all help it—after I take the throne, I still—still…"

And he said no more.

And she still couldn't get why he'd felt the need to push her away.

Had he thought she'd expected commitment from him and pushed her away because he couldn't promise any? Didn't he know she'd never entertained the possibility, even when she'd thought he was only one of the many thousands of royals around?

The only explanation was that he had no idea what she thought, and his acute sense of honor had refused to raise her hopes in vain. Or maybe he knew she'd realized all she could ever have with him would be fleeting yet felt he owed his destined status more caution and the wife looming in his future more fidelity.

Whatever he thought, it distressed him. And she wanted to release him, give him peace. She tried to.

"Malek, I—I ache for your loss, for your burdens. I sensed them, wanted to do all I could to make them hurt less that day when we came back from Mejbel. But that's all I wanted. I never expected anything in return—or anything at all. Believe me. You don't need to explain your obligations or feel bad about me or about anything you did. You never led me on."

He rumbled something harsh, laden in fury and disbelief. "I didn't? Strange. I led myself on."

A gasp scraped her throat. What did he mean?

"I led myself on all the way," he growled, turning on her, ferocity blasting off him. "All the damned way to no return."

Oh, God. Is he saying he—he feels the same?

No, he couldn't. He couldn't possibly have fallen in love, too.

Yes, love. Far beyond love. She hadn't dared name the immense, all-consuming feelings she had for him, which had been building since the first moment she'd laid eyes on him, wishing to keep even a shred of herself un-surrendered. But it had been an exercise in futility. Reality would have remained the same no matter the lack of label or the escape from self-confrontation.

"Malek—don't..." She had no idea what she wanted to say. Elation and desperation were hacking away at her, and she couldn't bear that he'd be feeling the same.

He wouldn't let her find words. He snatched her off her feet, making her feel weightless, powerless, soaring, then his arms pulled her against his hardness, crushed her to his chest where she'd dreamed of being.

She moaned her surrender, her greed, her welcome, clawed back at him. He took her to the trailer's wall, pushed her against it, dominated her. But he was also a supplicant, worshipping, devouring, his lips wrenching hot, blind, desperate kisses from hers, every convulsive press of his hands, every molten glide of his lips, every invasive thrust of his tongue showing her how much—just *how much*—she would be losing. Would never have.

But she had it, him, *now*. He was there, losing himself in her. She had to hoard all she could of him.

She'd barely started when he tore his lips away. She cried out, surged up, desperate for his breath so she could breathe, for his heartbeat so her heart wouldn't stop, needing one more plunge into his taste and potency to fill up for the desolate future without him.

He thwarted her, his hands shackles on her shoulders holding her off, his face contorted in agony. Her hungry sobs became ones of answering agony, tears that felt like acid eating their way out of her eyes and down her face.

The sight of her tears seemed to snap something inside him, and with a rumble of surrender the tension holding him away deflated, bringing his proud head down to hers with a dark groan, pressing, rubbing his longing.

He let her drag him down, only to graze her lips in an open-mouthed kiss before burying them, and his whole face, into her neck, her breasts, his growls of enjoyment and suffering elemental, jolts of molten agony to her core. And that was before his thick, ragged confessions tore into her.

"Ahebek ya rohi, ya galbi, ya agli—k'm ahebbek, k'm abghaki..."

Oh, God, was he saying he loved her? That she was his soul, his heart and mind—how he loved her, craved her…?

And it didn't matter what came next. She had to convince him that it didn't. Nothing did. He loved her now. She knew he did. With all his indomitable, magnificent being he did. For now. And she wanted to have every spark of it, of him. For as long as possible. If even for one day. One hour. She wanted it. Needed it. Had to have it.

She started struggling in his arms for more, opening herself up, offering all she had, all she was. She frantically locked her legs around him. She arched back on a wild moan with the feel of his hard hips filling her legs' hug as his muscled bulk filled her arms', with the feel of his erection pressing into her core, daunting, assuaging even through the barrier of clothes. She pressed his head harder, leading him to her bursting breasts, and with another growl of voracity he gave in, opened his mouth over her sweatshirt-smothered flesh, bit into it. She screamed, bucked with the slam of pleasure, losing what remained of her coherence with wanting more. He gave her more.

He pinpointed her nipples, nipped and suckled through her clothes until her moans became keens. Then he came up, devoured her vocal, irrevocable confession of need, of surrender, his tongue plunging inside her mouth, filling her, mating with hers, each slide spearing ecstasy to her core, each thrust layering arousal until her tears poured again, unable to withstand the build-up. He was as lost as her now, a constant rumble echoing in his chest. He ground his erection into her, simulating the plunging she was burning for. She writhed in his arms, snatched at him, lost, mad, blackness frothing from the periphery of her vision, a storm front of pleasure and suffering advancing from her core, where he was so near, so far.

She sobbed it all in his mouth. "I love you, Malek, love you—just take me—just make me yours, oh, please, please…"

He jerked up, staggered away, leaving her to crumple to the floor without his support.

She sank in a heap of mortification, his rejection hacking at her. But it was the look of horror and contrition on his face that hurt most.

He sagged down on her bed, as if he couldn't stand any more, in every way. He dropped his head into his hands. His distress poured strength into her limbs, made her lurch up to her feet, rush to his side, trying to contain it in her hug.

He shook his head, groaned, "*Aasef habibati, aasef-ya Ullah*—I'm so sorry. I shouldn't have…"

She hugged him harder. "Don't, Malek. I just want to love you. I never for one second thought you could be mine, in any way, but I just want to be yours."

He shook her arms off him, his eyes boring into her, incensed. "*No.* Don't offer, Janaan, don't be a fool. It doesn't matter that I'll always be yours in my heart. I'll never be yours where and how it matters. Do you understand?"

She'd always understood. But she understood something new now. She was compounding his burdens, tearing at his heart, compromising his sanity. Just by being near, she might destroy him. She'd die first. She must leave him alone. And she would.

This time she knew what she'd say. "Don't do this to yourself. I can't see you so—so anguished. I'll leave Damhoor, and you'll forget me."

He gave a short, savage laugh. "*Aih,* right after I forget myself. When I said *rohi wa galbi wa agli ya, Janaan,* I wasn't plying you with sweet nothings. I've never said those things, and I'll never say them again to another. You *are* your name, *ya hayati*, you've become my very soul and heart and mind."

When would the pain reach its peak?

"You—you don't know what you'll feel a month from now, a year. Time will—"

"Time and duty and another woman will only plunge me into a lifetime of withdrawal, will destroy my spirit with deprivation."

"But I don't want that." She almost screamed it. "Don't make me hate myself for being the reason for all this. You have so much to live for, so much to give so many people. I don't matter. What happens to me doesn't matter."

Malek stared at her, love tearing at him, demanding fulfillment, surrender. Then her words registered and a tidal wave of dread inundated him.

Could she, like her mother, love too much, destroy herself with the force of her desperation? Could she end up harming herself, snuffing out her life? *Ya Ullah, laa, laa!*

His hands sank into her flesh, shook her, as if he'd jog her back from the brink of an abyss. "Never—*never, ever* say, ever *think* anything so insane. I forbid you, do you hear me? You matter, you matter more than anything!"

She almost smiled at him, as if reading his fear, letting him know how far-fetched it was. But was it? Was it?

He could swear he heard his heart fracturing when she smoothed his hair, leaned her head on his shoulder and murmured, "I'm just telling you that you have more important things to think about, a whole country, and more, sooner or later. I don't matter compared to that. I—I just want you to fulfill your destiny and be happy…"

Before he could rave he'd never be anything but miserable for the rest of his dismal life, she pushed away, swayed up to her feet. "Just go now, Malek. Please, arrange for my return to Halwan at once. I'll leave Damhoor and you won't see or hear from me again. I'll never cause you discomfort."

He exploded to his feet. "Discomfort? Discomfort?"

His storming footsteps came to an abrupt end. He had to end this. He was damaging her further. He had to deliver the words that had been gathering like a storm inside him ever since he'd known he loved her and would have to give her up.

"*Ya habibati—ya hayati, ana—ana…*" He stopped, struggled to bring his voice, his emotions under control. "I may not be able to give you all of me, but you have all my love. *All* of it. And you will have all my support, all through your life."

She gaped up at him. "Support? You mean…"

He nodded. "Everything you need to be in absolute comfort and security, you and anyone you want, will be yours."

"Are you talking about money?"

"Anything—and everything you'll ever need or want."

She lowered her eyes for a long moment, until he thought she wouldn't comment, had accepted. Then she raised her eyes to him, hard eyes, and, *ya Ullah*, so hurt.

"I'm going to say this once. Once, Malek. I don't want, and I will never take, anything from you. Never. So don't ever, ever say this again, and never, ever try to—to…"

She fell silent, breathing hard, her fists clamped at her sides. And he lost what remained of his mind.

He put his insanity into words. "Don't go, Janaan."

Her eyes flared, hesitant, raw.

"I can't take...what you offered." Her eyes dimmed again. He gritted his teeth. "But you came here to explore your heritage, and you've barely begun. I can't let this experience be a total loss for you just because you had the gross misfortune to meet me. Stay and continue doing the job you so love, that you do so magnificently well. Stay and let me show you your land."

She bowed her head, tore at his heart with her anguish, with everything that made her herself. Then she nodded. His heart almost blasted through his ribcage, to throw itself at her feet.

Her smile trembled up at him. "You know what? It may be a

good plan. On longer exposure you may find out I'm a boring, aggravating pain, and I may find out you're an overbearing, overgrown brat, and when it's over we'll be glad that it is…"

And she was in his arms again, his lips devouring her flippant words.

It was when they were both writhing in agony that he drew back, his every nerve cursing him for the deprivation.

"This is the last kiss, Janaan," he panted. "I'll keep my promise from now on."

She clung to him. "Even if I don't want you to? I don't want you to! Malek, please!"

He took himself out of reach at the cost of yet another portion of his soul, groaned, "Especially as you don't want me to. I have to protect you as you don't know the first thing about protecting yourself."

CHAPTER THIRTEEN

IT HAD BEEN A crazy plan.

One hatched by a clearly unbalanced mind and agreed upon by another mind in an equal state of disrepair.

To have more time together, in the same proximity and interaction of their first week together wasn't only crazy, it was heart-shredding, sanity-compromising, self-destructive.

It was also glorious. As they carried on their mission, traveled into the mountainous parts of Ashgoon, their rapport deepened, their appreciation of everything about each other soared. Malek was astounded by how right everything was. Their ideologies meshed, their wits, their senses of humor, their work ethic. Even the friction was magnificent.

She objected fiercely to his protective ways, called it his sheikh shtick, his terminally chauvinistic streak, and he was driven to distraction by her overly independent, if very effective, ways. They clashed, collaborated, melded, and it was beyond anything he'd ever dreamed of.

Beyond love and need, the concept of soulmates, one he'd only ever scoffed at, floated constantly in his mind, descending into his heart to become a fact. It explained how fast they'd both recognized and surrendered to their unprecedented connection.

But what wrecked him was her acceptance. That he'd never be hers, that she'd disappear from his life at the end of this mission. She had this serenity about her of someone who'd accepted her fate.

And as he counted down to the unthinkable day when he would have to let her go, knowing he'd hurt her as much as he'd hurt himself, knowing she'd go on hurting as much as he would, he couldn't stop marveling at how she seemed to have stopped thinking about what would happen next and threw herself into the here and now of this once-in-a-lifetime experience.

"So what do you intend to do from now on?"

It was only when she spoke that he realized he'd been staring at her.

"Hel-lo? Earth to deep-space Sheikh. Any hope you'll get the future king back on line?"

She was making fun of him. He loved it, as always. Also he loved how she didn't avoid talking about his status, had turned it into a subject for light-heartedness, sometimes even gentle ridicule, so it wouldn't overwhelm him, and her, with its inescapability.

But she'd asked him something. About the future, his plans for it.

Ya Ullah, she wanted projections of his life in the luxurious prison of duties he'd been sentenced to? Of his life with the faceless woman he'd take for a wife, force himself to touch, to copulate with…?

He stomach churned. He barely suppressed a shudder of revulsion and said abruptly, "What exactly do you want to know?"

She winced. "Whoa! You mentioned you have ongoing relief plans for the communities we visit, and I'm only curious to know what they are."

That was what she'd meant?

Of course. She hadn't intruded by question or comment into anything remotely personal.

No. No, that wasn't accurate. She did delve into his innermost recesses, his views, reactions, instincts, preferences, seemed to know them any way down to the last detail. She was avid to know everything that made him himself. But nothing about what made him a sheikh, or Damhoor's future king.

"OK, your chance to answer my most relevant question is over," she quipped. "Here comes the next wave of patients."

He blinked, turned his head to see children coming in.

Janaan rose from his side to organize them for examination by a quick triage. He'd barely shaken himself from his daze when she turned to him.

"These eight kids." She pointed to the ones she was leading to the examination stations as the others walked the rest out. "I suspect congenital heart conditions. Serious ones."

A quick look told him she was right. The children, between four and eight, looked nothing like their healthier counterparts. Emaciated, underdeveloped, subdued. Their labored breathing at rest and their blue-tinged lips and nails told the rest of the story. And to think those were the ones who'd survived. Others with more serious conditions had long since died when they could have been saved if only the necessary medical services had reached them.

But those children's families weren't living in the hostile mountains of Ashgoon out of choice. They were escapees from the civil wars, subsisting in inhuman conditions. What he and GAO were doing here was a drop in the ocean. He hoped enough drops would become a healing shower, prayed he'd have the wisdom to deal with this country's rulers, to one day solve these people's ongoing problems.

Jay joined their two internists in their exam. He joined her in examining the youngest two children.

He prepared the ECG machine while she did her exams. She lowered her stethoscope and beckoned to him as she cooed to the two little girls with a smile. He wheeled the machine forward, started joking with the little ones, who Jay informed him were Zahrah and Azzah, making a game of applying the gel to their emaciated chests. Jay joined in, turned placing the ECG electrodes and leads into more fun.

When they had the tracings they dressed the girls and he rushed to his bag, came back with huge chocolate bars to the delightful sound of the little girls' giggling. Jay was performing magic tricks for them!

With his heart booming at yet another of her surprises, being the Arabic speaker, it fell to him to be the one to disappoint the little girls by telling them they'd have to eat the chocolate after they got better, but that it would be soon, and there'd be way more then. They agreed to stay in bed until their friends were examined, then they'd take care of them all.

As they waited for the others to finish, he took Janaan aside. "How did you do that trick with the tongue depressor?"

Jay gave him a look of exaggerated self-importance and mystery. "You expect a magician to reveal her secrets? Tsk."

"I *know* you're a sorceress." He believed it. Look how she'd enchanted him, enslaved him. "But that *was* a trick—for a change. I'll trade you its secret for a rundown of my plans."

"No deal. I can find out your plans on my own."

He sighed. "Tormentor. *Zain*, I concede I'm no position to bargain." He soaked up her triumphant smile, smiled back. "So—my plans. I have definite ones for the communities under Damhoorian sovereignty. I'll provide them with comprehensive medical insurance and set up centers close enough to be within reach but far enough away so as not to encroach on their way of life, to serve as permanent medical and community services facilities. GAO will handle the logistics. I'll provide what they recommend."

She gave him one of those glances that made him feel he could spread his arms and fly.

"What about the communities outside Damhoor?" she asked.

That brought him crashing back to earth. "Those are another matter," he growled. "For instance, the Ashgoonian government welcomes my efforts as long as they're in a crisis or when they think it's those of a pampered royal playing at philanthropy. Once I put forward plans for the widespread reforms I have in mind, I doubt they'll be as grateful. Beyond medical services, these people need aggressive development programs to make their neighborhoods habitable, livestock, farming and small projects to help them become self-supporting, vocational training to provide them with desperately needed job skills and educational projects to break the cycle of ignorance and poverty."

Her eyes now made him feel as if he could single-handedly do all that. If he had her at his side, he knew he would…

"Skeikh Malek, we're ready to review our findings."

Malek shook himself from another attack of searing longing, turned to Mel Kawolski, their sole GAO cardiologist. "Go ahead."

"All six children are suffering from serious congenital heart defects and congestive heart failure," Mel said.

Malek nodded. "So are Zahrah and Azzah over there. Both are suffering from severe Fallot's tetralogy."

The other internist, Hal Zuckerman said, "We diagnosed two cases of severe coarctation of the aorta, three quite large ventricular septal defects, and one total mitral valve prolapse. They're all conditions necessitating surgical treatment."

Malek took one more look at the children who lay on their beds, fragile, helpless, looking at him as if they understood he was the one who had their fates in his hands.

He gritted his teeth. "Get me films, prepare the children and transfer them in order of severity to surgery." Mel nodded, got busy at once. Malek looked down at Jay. "Coming?"

She tore her gaze from the children, turned glittering eyes up at him. "Try to stop me."

She fell into brisk step with him as they exited the tent, traversed the clearance they'd made for their camp in the crowded, squalid mountain community. It was a fifteen-minute hike down to the valley where they'd left their convoy. Only the Jeeps had made it up the narrow, unpaved mountain roads.

As they reached the surgery trailer she paused at its steps. "I've been thinking, Malek. Maybe the Ashgoonian government will resist you now, but once you're king you will have far more power, and even if you can't influence them to put an end to these people's ordeals, you will be able to pressure them to let you intervene yourself. God—what a blessing that kind of power will be in your hands."

The permanent spasm behind his ribs sank talons into his heart, almost drove him to his knees.

"Janaan, this was a horrible idea…"

He bit his lip, barely stopped himself from ramming his head against the trailer's steel side.

Of all the stupid, insensitive things to say.

"Not letting me go when I asked to?" she completed for him. "Probably. But I stand by my words weeks ago. Coming here, getting to know you, *is* my life's most incredible experience, and I wouldn't wish it away for the world. I only hope you don't regret it too much." She suddenly poked him in the arm, grinned. "Now, lighten up, and power up on that healing magic of yours."

He swallowed the burning coal that had replaced his larynx as he followed her inside the trailer.

She hadn't fooled him with her levity. Every second she was beside him kept breaking her heart into smaller pieces. By the time she left it would be pulverized. As would his be.

It was five days later when their last batch of post-operative patients was airlifted to Halwan. Malek believed all the kids would make full recoveries. Now, with the rest of their medical and community services targets reached, it was time to move on to their next destination.

As they waited for the Jeeps to come down from the mountain, Jay watched everyone gearing up for the move.

She'd loved every heart-wrenching, fascinating, exhausting

second of the past three weeks, had come to know so much about the region and the people, had made friends and gained invaluable experience and knowledge. Then had come being with Malek. It had made everything that had happened between them before pale by comparison. She hadn't lied when she'd said the whole experience was and would remain her life's high point.

The bottom line was she'd been crazy to prolong her torment.

She'd long acknowledged she'd fallen in love with Malek during those first few hours, but extending her knowledge of him, prolonging the exposure, the glorious interaction, deepening the soul-deep bond had been an act of sheer lunacy.

She'd had a chance of surviving without him before those weeks. She'd thrown it away.

She stood staring sightlessly as the Jeeps made their way down the mountain, numb, burning despair seeping into her as she made the decision to walk away, today.

Suddenly she was distracted as if from the depths of a nightmare as one of their Jeeps lurched as the ground beneath it gave way. The driver tried to veer off the collapsing slice of mountain, failed and tilted sideways, over and over and over down the ravine leading to where they were.

The moment it crashed a dozen hundred feet away, chaos erupted. Screams, dozens of people running towards the crash, Malek ahead of everyone, his shouts drowning everyone else's with orders and directions, his speed outstripping them all.

She was running, too, her mind streaking ahead.

Get emergency bag. Prepare for the worst. Take charge. This is your turf.

She came back from fetching her bag to see Malek on top of the Jeep, sending everyone running back to fetch all they'd need to extract their people from the crumpled mess. She got nearer, her eyes riveted on him as he knocked in the remainder of the windshield to get to the injured inside. And then she saw it.

A boulder rolling down the mountain, right at him.

White noise exploded inside her skull, flooded her limbs with the power of desperation. She dimly felt she'd fly, as she needed to, to reach him, to shield him.

Then she did reach him, shielded him.

That knowledge and the detonation of all-encompassing pain were the last things she registered…

Malek heard the uproar rising again over the strident panting filling his ears. The sheer panic congealing his blood told him it was about Jay.

He wrenched around, saw it all at once.

Jay streaking towards him, her face a panicked, manic mask. The boulder he wouldn't be able to outrun. Janaan stopping in its path up the slope. The boulder hitting her with the speed of a racing car, knocking her down and rolling right on top of her before it hit the Jeep, its momentum almost spent. Spent against Janaan's body. *Her body.*

And suddenly he was flying, swooping down on her, her name an endless roar erupting from his chest, pouring from his eyes. *Janaan.*

Lying there broken. Because of him. And he wouldn't be able to reach her. Like he hadn't been able to reach Majd…

"Sheikh Malek."

He heard the shouted admonition. Felt the strong hands trying to snatch him back from the precipice of madness.

"Sheikh Malek, she needs you now. *She needs you.*"

Saeed. His right hand. Right now, his right mind. He'd just said the only thing that could wrench him out of the vortex of despair, the incapacitation of horror and guilt.

Janaan needed him. He couldn't afford to lose his mind, or have a stroke. He'd succumb to either, or both, only when he'd taken care of her, when he'd saved her.

"Sheikh Malek, we can take care of her from here…"

His roared "*No!*" silenced whomever had dared suggest

anyone but he would care for her. Only he would fight for her. No one else. Ever.

He reached a quaking hand to her carotid. She was alive.

He knelt over her, kissed her all over her swelling face, mixed his tears with her blood, murmured his pledge, "I'm here, *ya habibati*. I will never leave you. Never."

CHAPTER FOURTEEN

JANAAN WOKE UP in heaven.

She'd woken up many times before. Hazy, distorted times, in the mobile surgery unit's IC, in a different and far larger IC, in a hospital bed somewhere huge, ultra-modern and soothingly lit. The only constant she was sure she saw was Malek. In her delirium, in her episodes of distressing semi-wakefulness. Pouring caring, healing and love over her. He looked so haggard, so stricken, she wept. She couldn't see him this way.

She thought there was a stretch of time, the last she remembered, when she had been awake and talking. To him, to Hessuh, Saeed and Rafeeq. She remembered it as if she were remembering a half-forgotten movie. As if it hadn't been her sitting in that hospital bed. She remembered she'd wondered why she was there.

Now, as she opened her eyes to find herself draped in an ethereal cocoon of gossamer curtains cascading from a golden frame, and felt herself drowning in the luxurious depths of sheerest white and softest cotton, drenched in nerve-tingling spicy scents, warmth and mellow sunlight, she remembered why.

She'd hurtled into the path of a thundering boulder.

Judging by the persistent IC themes, it must have shattered her. Judging by Malek's constant presence, it must have been him who'd put her back together.

"I will have to lock you up."

Malek. His voice as dark and haggard as she remembered he'd looked in her delirium.

She twisted around, homing in on it. She found him two feet away on the other side of the gigantic bed, sprawled in a huge, high-backed armchair, his legs wide apart.

Through the gauzy curtain she saw he was wearing an *abaya,* white and embroidered with gold all along its opposing openings.

It was the first time she'd seen him in traditional garb. He looked regal, overwhelming in anything, but in this, he was… Whoa. He was just…just… *Whoa.*

This was what he was born to wear. Her incomparable prince of the desert.

He stood up in one of those flowing moves that never ceased to stun her, with him being so big and tall, and the *abaya* fell open. And she had her first unhindered view of his body.

She should have known that all the fantasies that had tormented her in endless nights of deprivation would be nothing to his reality. It had been merciful she hadn't had enough imagination to do him justice.

She didn't need imagination now. Would never need it again. From now on she'd have memory. Of the chest she'd longed to lose herself against, a painstaking sculpture of perfection and potency, dusted in just the exact thickness of ebony silk to accentuate each slope and bulge of sheer maleness, to offset polished flesh, before the tantalizing layer arrowed down over an abdomen hewn from living granite by virility gods and endless stamina and discipline. Below that, string-tied white pants straight out of a thousand and one Arabian nights hung low, way low, on those narrow, muscled hips and those formidable thighs, the loose cut doing nothing to hide the shape and size of his briefs-bridled manhood.

She couldn't breathe. Her insides cramped with a blow of longing so hard she moaned.

At hearing the explicit sound his eyes flared like a sun going supernova. "But it won't be enough. Only chaining you to my wrist and throwing away the key will be."

And he considered that—what? Punishment?

She tried to talk, found that sandpaper had replaced her vocal cords.

"Feeling the after-effects of intubation still?" He placed one knee on the bed, making the hard mattress dip, putting his hands to the curtains as if he was feeling walls he was about to smash, his pose imposing, intimidating. And even more arousing. At least she knew her body was functioning if it was rioting this way, when he was clearly furious, too. "That's what you get for playing Superwoman. Surprise. The boulder didn't bounce off you."

She found her voice for this, or something that passed for it. "As long as it didn't hit you."

He tore the curtains away, loomed over her, panting, his skin turning copper in his extreme. Oh, God, what had she said?

"And why would you care, when you almost killed me anyway? Seeing you lying there, broken and bloody! The one reason I didn't keel over was because I had to take care of you first. Because you were alive. If you weren't—if..." He clenched and unclenched his fists, as if he was struggling not to grab her and shake her. "You could have just shouted for me to get out of the way. You could...you could... *Be'hag Ellahi...*you could have *died.*"

"That's why you're so angry?" Tension seeped out of her. "I thought it was something serious."

"Almost killing yourself isn't serious?" he exploded.

She winced at his thundering volume. "Endangering myself is one of your hot buttons, isn't it?"

"*One* of?" She'd bet that snarl could perforate steel. "*Endangering* yourself? You risked your life for mine!"

She ran her hands over her head, her arms. "Uh, I feel very much alive here. Not withstanding that my first thought as I woke up here was that I must be in heaven."

"You risked your *life* for *mine*. That you're still alive is because God chose not to accept your sacrifice."

"I think you had a say in canceling that sacrifice." She sat up and he seemed to lose all explosive retorts in his alarm over her sudden move. "Oh, I'm all right. As good as new, really, just sore from lying in bed too…" Her words petered out. She was in a sleeveless, low-cut, satin nightdress the same dazzling white as everything around her.

Her heat rose as she imagined him putting her in it, and more as she, in such languorous detail, saw him taking her out of it. A breath shuddered out of her as the creamy silk slid over her legs, intensifying the heavy throb between them.

She squeezed them together to contain the ache, looked up at him with eyes barely open with the weight of desire.

"So, how bad was it?" she almost moaned.

Malek's teeth clapped together before grinding out a sound that made her dizzy. "Severe concussion, scalp wound, six badly bruised ribs, lacerated intercostals muscles, collapsed lung, massive hemopneumothorax. And a full body contusion."

"In other words, I got off pretty lightly."

"Lightly? Do you want to rid me of what little remains of my sanity? It was only because of that monster emergency bag you so love, which you held up as a shield at the last moment, that you're not dead. Or, worse, maimed beyond recognition, a paralyzed vegetable!"

"Well, I'm not. You saved me."

"Only because you saved me."

"So what do you say we call it even? We are, really." Before he could rave and rant again she hurried on, "And just where are we? Is this your home?"

He scowled his displeasure at her change of subject and muttered, "We are in Ayn Al-Hayah oasis. I have a retreat here."

"An oasis! So I wasn't that far off when I thought I was in heaven. Ayn Al-Hayah." She sighed, felt a sore spot where he must have placed a chest tube to drain accumulating blood inside her chest. "Eye of life?"

"*Ayn* here means spring."

"Hmm. So how long have we been here?"

His scowl softened, his eyes turning amber with deflating anger and mounting awareness. "Just today. You were in and out of consciousness for nineteen days before that."

"I've been in la-la-land for *twenty* days?"

"Which part of severe concussion didn't you get? And then you were in pain, and I had you on potent painkillers, and those knocked you out even worse than the concussion did. You'd look awake and then I'd later realize that you had been sleep-talking."

"Yeah, my threshold to any kind of medication is low. But what about the mission?"

"*Elal Jaheem* with the mission." That was roared. "You're thinking of the mission when it's a miracle that you're alive?"

"Well, *duh*. Of course..." She suddenly sat up. "The people in the Jeep...what happened to them?"

His eyes remained hard, but his voice gentled. "Another batch of miracles. Fractures and concussions and gashes but nothing too serious."

She subsided against her downy pillow. "Thank God."

His tension eased, his eyes melted. He came down on the bed, supported by his extended arm. And it hit her harder. The scent of maleness and protectiveness, fiery and clean and musky. Her mouth watered. Her stomach rumbled.

"You're hungry." He started to get up and she clutched his hand. The hand that had snatched her from death's jaws.

"Not for food." She pulled at it, bringing his unresisting bulk down to her. "Not for food, *ya habibi*."

"Janaan..." he groaned as he sank in her arms, letting her singe her lips with the pleasure of running them all over his jaw, his neck, his cheekbones.

"You shaved for me," she moaned into his skin. "You knew I'd wake up starving for you, wanted me to feast on you."

And she tried, trembling with the enormity of having him in her arms again, her hands quaking over the breadth of his back, the leashed power of his arms, sinking in the knotted muscles, in his vitality, his reality, her lips taking hesitant glides over his, her tongue laving them in tiny licks, still not believing their texture and taste.

A rumble poured into her mouth, lancing into her heart just as it spiked her arousal to pain with its unadulterated passion.

Then he broke away from her.

She felt as if he'd backhanded her, fell back onto her pillow, gasping, her eyes gushing her misery.

He was panting, his face taut with agony. Then the words shuddered out of him. "Nothing has changed, *ya hayati.*"

A sob overcame her as she tried to reach for him again. He resisted her. This time his rejection clamped her chest with the frost of suspicion.

Stone cold, she got out of bed on unsteady legs. "You've researched me, haven't you? You're afraid getting involved with me, even temporarily, an illegitimate daughter and half-sister to Damhoorian men of ill repute would be too damaging…"

He exploded to his feet, his rage rattling her teeth.

"Enti majnoonah?" he thundered. "Are you totally crazy, or is this the drugs talking? You think I'd care if you were *Al Shy'taan's*—Satan's—daughter? And afraid of *getting involved*? *The whole kingdom* is certain you *are* my mistress. I spent a night in your hotel room. The whole mission saw me weeping and roaring for you. I brought you here, put you in my bed. And you think I care what the world says or thinks? You think I'm denying you and myself for those petty reasons?"

"Then why?" she cried. "The only other reason I can think of is you don't want me any more."

He advanced on her, forcing her to stumble backward with his insistent momentum, until he had her plastered to the wall.

Then he showed her just how huge his desire was, how much he wanted her.

"Is this proof enough for you, *ya majnoonah*? And beyond going insane with lusting for your every inch, I worship you, I crave your every glance and word and thought and emotion—*everything* that makes you you."

She clung to him and he stepped away, thwarting her. She cried out her confusion, "Then why won't you have mercy on me?"

"Because I still don't have the right to choose my wife."

Wife.

And it came to her. Fully formed. What she'd never allowed herself to even think about. The images, the daily details, every sensation and thought and common occurrence of an existence as his wife. It brought a fresh wave of anguish. She sobbed as if her heart would break.

He snatched her up in his arms, carried her to bed, curved himself around her. "*Domoo'ek aghla men hayati*—your tears *are* more precious than my life, *ya galbi, argooki*, don't cry."

It was only on account of hearing his voice about to fracture that she found the control to leash in her anguish.

"I never thought I was qualified to be your wife—" she started.

He cut her off with a snarl. "You *are* my wife. In my heart and soul. But because I can't choose you, I can never have one. And I won't."

The way he'd said that…! "You mean…?"

"I'll take the crown but I will not take a wife."

"B-but how can you not? The heir you need, the expectations of the whole kingdom…"

"I'm not having a child if it isn't with you. Let the crown go to someone else after me."

This was—was too much. *Too much.* Too *huge.*

She felt shock relinquish its choke hold on her every cell, heard herself stammering, "But i-if you d-decided that, how can you say that nothing has changed? Everything has!"

"*Nothing* has. I still can't take you as my wife."

"You don't have to! I only ever wanted to be with you for as long as you didn't have a wife. And if you won't, I can be with you forever…" She stopped, mortification rising at her presumption. "F-for as long as you want me."

"And what will I give you in return? Will you accept sharing my privileges?"

Her lips pursed. "We've covered this, once and for all."

"So if you won't accept my support and protection, what do I have to offer you? My love? My body?"

A giggle of incredulity ripped out of her chest. "Is there anything more this life can offer?"

"No, Janaan. You of all people need more than someone who says he loves you and never delivers."

"If you're alluding to my father, there is just no comparison. My father deserted my mother and me for—what did you call them? Self-preserving, petty reasons. While you—"

His growl interrupted her. "It doesn't matter how grand my reasons are. I can't let you invest yourself, body and soul, as I know you would, in a relationship with no future. You need a man who can give you the family you never had, the family you of all women were born to nurture and cherish. Damn the day I was born, but I can't be that man."

Jay felt her sanity ebbing. Malek was in her arms, telling her he'd never take another woman, that he'd love her forever, but he wouldn't be hers either.

"You think you're protecting me? Don't you see you're hurting me, destroying me?"

"The pain of an hour rather than that of every hour, as we say here. You may never forgive me for being unable to be with you, for crushing your heart as I crushed mine, but you'll remember I didn't compound your involvement, your addiction…"

She struggled out of his arms, looked at him with tears pouring down her face. "I could have died, Malek."

His reaction was spectacular. As if she'd shot him point-blank in the chest.

And it all gushed out of her. "I could have died without having lived. I haven't lived, Malek, because you won't let me, because you won't make me yours. What if I die tomorrow? Be gone in seconds, like Majd? Won't you let me live now?"

Jan's words showered Malek like shrapnel. He could swear he heard them slashing the last of his control, snapping it.

He surged up, blind, out of his mind, reliving the agony of fear, of helplessness, of rage and regret. He caught her to him, filled his hands with her, honey and sunlight and unconditional love made flesh, made woman, all woman. His woman.

"Ana ella ensan," he growled in her mouth, between tongue thrusts that breached the sweetness she surrendered with such mind-destroying eagerness. "I'm only human…"

He tore his lips away and she whimpered. He only sank worshiping kisses all the way down to her ample cleavage.

"You're not pulling away?" she gasped.

"Never again," he groaned, suckling her honeyed flesh. "There'll be no turning back. I'll worship you, brand you, give you all of me, turn your body into an instrument of ecstasy, yours and mine. You're mine to pleasure as I will, aren't you?"

Her nod was frantic. "Yes, yes. I'm yours. Yours. Love me, *ya habibi*, show me what being alive feels like."

He fell to his haunches under the import, the conviction of her words, groaning, *"Maboodati…"*

He bunched her nightdress in his fists, looked up at his goddess, peach-flushed, eyes almost black, the totality of her hunger and trust shooting to his heart, tampering with its rhythm, crimson lips swollen with his passion, panting for more, beckoning him to lose his mind, once and for all.

He raised the nightdress up, exposing her an inch at a time, replacing it with his lips, tongue, teeth, coating her velvet firmness in suckles and nibbles, knowing just where to skim and tantalize, where to linger and torment, where to draw harder and devour. Her moans became cries, then keens, then loud, labored gasps.

The pressure in his loins was reaching unbearable levels until he feared the first time wouldn't be the languorous seduction he'd hoped it would be. The accumulation of need had reached critical levels and it would be like a dam breaking the moment he thrust inside her.

No. He couldn't let her first intimacy with him be anything less than perfect bliss. He had to show her what she meant to him. Show her he craved her pleasure far more than he craved his own, that his pleasure stemmed from hers.

Yes. He'd show her how he cherished her, what he'd give, what he'd endure to give her the best, give her everything. Always.

Her nightdress was now past her midriff, past her ability to stand the sensual torment. He took pity on her, straightened, taking the nightdress with him, over her breasts, over her head.

He stood back, took his first gulp of her, exposed but for the lacy morsel Hessuh had helped Janaan put on before he'd brought her here, and almost dropped to his knees again.

He'd seen parts of her as he'd treated her, but he'd been out of his mind with fear, his surgeon side in full control. Now he saw her as a woman, not a patient. And there she was. Beyond his fantasies. Ripe, strong, tailored to his every last fastidious taste and beyond. His woman. And she was dying for him, as he was for her, quaking with the force of her need, weeping with it.

Her arms stretched out in demand, in supplication, and sabotaged what was left of his reason.

He yanked her to him, bending her over one arm, her breasts an erotic offering. Pouring litanies of worship into her lips, all over her face, he kneaded, weighed one breast, seeking one erect, deep peach nipple, pinching and rolling it before he moved down, captured the other bud of overpowering femininity and need in his mouth, felt as if he'd captured a vital, missing part of his life's meaning.

She screamed. With each pull she screamed again, shuddered. His hands glided over her abdomen, shaking with the privilege, the freedom, closing over her trim mound, stilled in awe. This was his home. His home inside her. And she was letting him have it, own it. He squeezed his eyes, her flesh.

Just as she screamed again, he slid two fingers between the velvet slickness of her exquisite folds, spreading them, getting drunk with the scent of her arousal, the evidence of her love and dependence. She was ready for him.

He slipped a careful finger inside her, needing to know how much and went blind with another blast of arousal. Soaking, for him, but…so tight. And she lurched, as if he'd hurt her.

So not so ready for him. But ready for pleasure. And how he'd pleasure her.

He stroked her, spread honey from her slit before his fingers made way for his thumb to find the knot of flesh where her nerves converged, her trigger. The moment he touched it, he felt as if he'd touched the core of the sun, her cries of love, of his name, strangled and she bucked in his arms.

He roared with pride, swept her off her feet, deposited her with all the cherishing and gentleness pouring out of his being for her onto the bed, crashed to his knees in front of her, spreading her shaking legs, bringing them over his shoulders, his hands and lips and teeth devouring their every inch. Tension invaded her body again, until she was thrashing again.

"Malek, please…I n-need you…"

For answer, he spread her core, gave her one long lick. She bucked off the bed, screamed again. "Please, Malek…you… *you…*"

He subdued her with one hand flat on her abdomen. "Let me taste you, taste your pleasure," he begged. "I've been starving for you. Let me have my fill, give me everything you have."

She still tried to squeeze her legs closed, her eyes wet and beseeching. And he realized. She was shy!

Following on the heels of this realization came the certainty. No one had ever tasted her before. His wild flower of the desert had never allowed anyone this privilege! And she would give it to him. The privilege was his alone, now and forever.

He staked his claim. "Aren't you mine?"

She nodded mutely, her color high.

He surged up, dragged pillows, propped her up against them so she was half-sitting. He withdrew to look at his arrangement, Janaan, open and willing for his ministrations. Blood whooshed, a geyser in his head, in his erection. He gritted his teeth, watched her hands convulsing in the sheets, her body tensing up.

"Don't be shy, *ya hayati*. And don't close your eyes. Watch me worship you, pleasure you, own your every secret. Look me in the eye as I bring you to orgasm this time."

She squirmed, hiccupped. "Malek, I can't, please…"

"You can. You will." He latched onto her core. He drank her, her essence, her need, her pleasure. Then when he knew her body was screaming for release, he tongue-lashed her clitoris, and she shredded her throat on ecstasy, unraveled her body on a chain reaction of convulsions. And looked him in the eyes all through. It was the most erotic, most intimate, most fulfilling experience of his life.

But, then, every touch, every glance from her had been that. Now he'd take her, and union with her would reinvent the terms of eroticism, intimacy and fulfillment. He prayed she was ready enough now.

First, to bring her to fever pitch again.

He slid up her sweat-slick body, snatching the pillows from beneath her, flattening her to the bed, soaking up her drugged look, the looseness confessing the depth of her satisfaction.

But as soon as he branded her lips, letting her taste her pleasure on his, her breath hitched, her cool sweat evaporated on a blast of heat radiating from her core. She was aroused that much, that fast again? He hadn't even started stimulating her.

He withdrew to make sure, and she clutched at him, tearing the *abaya* from his shoulders. "I want to see you—all of you. Oh, please, I don't want pleasure—I want you, I'm dying to feel you, deep inside me, filling my body, please…"

Hearing the last pillar in his mind give, he snatched at her lips with rough, moist kisses, nothing left in him but the corrosive need to bury himself inside her, fill her, dominate her, surrender to her, knowing that it was what she needed too.

He heaved himself up, tore off his *abaya* and pants. She fell on her back, held out her arms, her eyes streaming her plea for him.

He surged back to her, covered her, felt her beloved flesh cushioning his hardness. She opened her legs and, as he'd long dreamed, he guided them over his waist.

He fused their lips for feverish seconds before he reared up, his eyes seeking hers, his erection seeking her entrance.

Finding both hot and molten, he growled his surrender, sank into her in one forceful thrust.

Home. *At last.* At last.

It was on the second thrust that he realized why the first one had taken such force, found such resistance, why her beloved body had bowed up in such rigid shock. Why his ears were still ringing with her scream.

She was a virgin.

CHAPTER FIFTEEN

SHE *HAD* BEEN a virgin.

Malek lay on top of Janaan, buried in her depths, the realization pummeling him, paralyzing him.

He should have known. It had all been there. The evidence of her innocence. From the first moment.

The shyness and wariness that had so contrasted with her efficiency and resolve. The pain at his experimental invasion while he'd pleasured her. Her unnerved reaction, even in her total willingness to offer him all she had, to the rest of the intimacies he'd lavished on her. Fool that he was, he'd thought she hadn't been tasted, when she hadn't been touched at all.

He was her first. And he'd hurt her. She now lay beneath him, quivering, her impossible tightness throbbing around his invasion, her torn innocence a new gush of heat singeing his flesh, and—God help him—arousing him to madness.

Ashamed, suffocating, unable to look her in the eye, he moved, started to withdraw his body from hers. Her sob tore through him. *Ya Ullah*, he'd hurt her. *Hurt her.*

But she was clamping quaking legs over his hips, stopping him from exiting her body, pumping her hips up, impaling herself further on his hardness, forcing him back inside her.

"I'm hurting you." He barely recognized the butchered protest that scratched the panting-filled silence as his.

"Yes—yes..." That made him heave up in horror. She only clung harder to him, arms and legs, her core clamping him like a hot fist. "It's *magnificent*...you are. I dreamed—but could have never dreamed you'd feel this way inside me. Oh, Malek, Malek, your heat and power, the pain and pleasure. *Habibi*, brand me, finish me..."

How many times could she wreck his sanity before it disintegrated irrevocably?

Helpless to do anything but her bidding, he thrust back into her, gentle this time, slow. She thrashed her head against the bed, bucking her hips beneath his, engulfing more of his near-bursting erection into her heat. "Don't hold back. Give it all to me. I'm yours, *ya habibi*, yours."

He rose, cupped her hips in his hands, tilted her and thrust himself to the hilt inside her.

He withdrew all the way out, looked down on the awesome sight of his shaft resting at her entrance then sank slowly inside her until he didn't see where he ended and she began.

He raised his eyes to hers, found her propped up on her elbows, watching, too, crimson lips swollen, open on frantic pants, eyes stunned, streaming, wild. He drew out, thrust again, and she collapsed back, crying out a hot gust of passion, opening wider for each thrust, an ecstatic amalgam of pain and pleasure slashing across her face, rippling through her body.

He kept his pace gentle, massaging her all over, bending to suckle her breasts, drain her lips, rain wonder all over her.

"See how beautiful you are? See how perfectly I fit inside you? See what you do to me? See what I'm doing to you?"

She writhed beneath him with every word, her hair blinding splashes of sunlight over the whiteness, her breathing becoming fevered snatches, her whole body straining at him, around him, making him pick up speed—though he managed to somehow not give in to his body's uproar for more force—her answering confessions getting more uninhibited.

Her honeyed depths started to ripple around him. He quickened his thrusts until she screamed, bucked, froze, then convulsion after convulsion squeezed screams out of her, clamped her tight inferno around his erection in wrenching spasms.

The force, the very sight and sound and knowledge of her release broke his dam. He roared, let go, his body all but detonating in ecstasy, his seed jetting endlessly into her, until he felt his essence flowing into her, never to return.

Shaking with the aftershocks of his life's most violent and profound release, he fought the need to come down on top of her, feel every inch of her along every inch of him. He'd tested her recuperating body enough.

He collapsed beside her, took her over him with extreme care, making sure he remained inside her.

She lay limp and cooling on top of him, the biggest part of his soul. He'd never known physical intimacy could be like this, channeling directly into his spirit, his reason. It had been a good thing he hadn't been anywhere near accurate imagining how sublime making love to her would be. He would have definitely lost his mind during the past weeks.

He encompassed her velvet firmness in caresses, letting the memories and sensations replay in his mind and body, letting awe overtake him.

He was her first. And she'd needed him so much that, even through her pain, he'd managed to give her pleasure.

Not that it would have mattered to him if she'd been experienced. He'd fallen in love with her believing she was, not for a minute thinking it his business, or questioning it with her age and culture. Even when she'd talked about her lack of involvement with men, he'd assumed she'd meant in a serious way.

But now he knew, he was just about bursting with pride—and shame.

Just as she'd offered her life for his when she'd believed he'd offer her nothing at all in return, she'd offered her innocence when she still believed the same.

And he had to tell her *now* that he'd been insane to think it possible to let her go. For any reason. She would have all of him, for as long as he lived. He'd make it so. Somehow.

"Janaan, *mashoogati*," he murmured into her hair as he pressed her into his body, satiation, gratitude, love and humility radiating from his very core. "I thought being with you the last weeks had been, and would remain, my life's most incredible, unrepeatable experience. And then you gave me this. Now I know every minute with you, every time in your arms, in your body and passion, will be that all over again and then more. And no matter what happens, I'm never giving you up. I'm never letting you down. I'll be the man to give you all you need and deserve. Forever."

Silence met his proclamation.

Didn't she believe him? Did she think it the empty promises of a man drunk on ecstasy, panting for more?

"Janaan…?"

The faintest snore answered his questioning whisper. Then she turned her face into his chest and her breath became soundless again. She was asleep!

Of course she was. It was another miracle she'd weathered all he'd put her through in the last hour.

He spread himself more, hoping to provide her with more comfort, dragged the cover over them, gathered her tighter in his arms. "Sleep, *ya maboodati*, get well. You will need all your strength when you wake up. For a very, very long future together."

He could swear she smiled in her sleep.

Jay woke up with a start. She realized one thing at once.

This time, she *was* in heaven.

She was wrapped in it. It was a huge desert lion of a man, the epitome of maleness and manhood and humanity. Malek.

His legs enveloped hers, one heavily muscled arm propping

him up on one elbow, the other cherishing her protectively around her waist. He was looking down at her with eyes that had replaced the sun in her world, his smile adoration, possession and barely leashed voracity.

Awareness burst inside her brain, bringing with it every single second and sensation of their union. Then he moved, a deceptively lazy shift bringing his legs around to massage hers, the arm at her waist taking her to his wide chest.

"Ma arwa'ek fee uhdani, ya maboodati." His bass rumble dripped with satisfaction. And just that edge of imperiousness that so befitted him.

"That made zero sense to me." She leaned back over his arm, for a more comprehensive view of the force of nature that had claimed her, transfigured her. The movement brought her breasts pressing into him. A fresh wave of heat drenched her. "And I thought I was getting good at Arabic."

"You are. I'm just saying things you'll never hear from anyone else. Where else but from my lips would you hear how magnificent you are in the depths of my embrace, my goddess?"

God—could he talk! As if he needed to enhance his hold on her.

"In one of those ancient desert poets' works?" she whispered, trying to bring her emotions to a manageable level.

"I've been becoming one ever since I laid eyes on you. I *am* this close to becoming your lunatic, like our history's most famous poet. But I'll go mad with too much unconditional love, rather than a thwarted, unrequited one."

And he wasn't even joking.

She had to lighten this up, before she made a fool of herself, weeping with the sheer beauty of it, of him, of the memories.

"I want this formidable mind of yours intact," she quipped. "Maybe on cessation of exposure, your condition will reverse?"

He pressed her into him more, his eyes flaring. "Don't even joke about it. Expose me, *ya mashoogati,* flay me with your love."

She looked at him, everything she'd never hoped to find, let alone have, spread beside her, beyond dreams and comprehension, surrendering his uniqueness to her to worship…

She hiccupped, buried her face in his chest.

"You're shy again?" He tried to bring her face up and she squirmed, dug deeper into him. "After you gave me what I never thought could be given, made me feel what I never thought could be felt? After you made me understand what it means to give one's all? You gave me your all, took mine, *ya hayati.*"

She nodded, tickling her nose on his chest hair. "Hence this bout of crippling shyness."

This made him put her away and sit up, a scowl knotting his brow. "You regret it?"

Her lips twisted. "Is it OK to scoff at a crown prince and a future king?" He raised one imposing eyebrow, reading her mischief, promising retribution for the anxiety the very thought of her regret had caused him. "But to tell the truth, shyness is always caused by naughty thoughts one is unable to handle."

"*Enti janaani*—you're my Janaan. You can handle anything. You can handle me. In every sense of the word."

And she dove into him, wrapping her arms around his endless back. "Love me again, Malek."

He growled deep in his chest, spread her back in bed, blazed down her body with hands and lips. She realized his intention and was overcome by another tidal wave of memories and embarrassment. She tried to keep her legs closed, but he insisted, caressed them apart.

"Open up yourself to me, let me feast, let me heal you…"

"I'm healed," she cried out. "Please…!"

"Your injuries, yes, but it will be pain unmixed with pleasure if I take you now." She started protesting, and one of those long, perfect fingers found her entrance. She lurched with a jolt of stimulation-laced burning. Then he dipped in, and each slow inch felt like a red-hot skewer driving deeper into inflamed tissue.

He held her eyes all through, drawing the admission that there was no way she'd accommodate him right now.

Then she looked down on his promise of endless pleasure lying daunting in length and thickness over his abdomen, and nothing mattered but having him inside her.

She tried to wrap her legs around him in silent supplication, and he only opened them fully, smiled his pledge, cherishing and carnal, burned it in licks and nibbles and ragged confessions down to her core. She collapsed, not one muscle functioning anymore as his magnificent head settled between her thighs and his lips and tongue soothed and scorched her sore flesh, the very heart of her secrets that she could surrender to no one but him.

She was lost again, and again, in the tumult of the body and soul-racking ecstasy he detonated in her depths, holding his eyes all through, as they demanded, as he needed her to.

Finally he came up, wrapped himself around her as she lay trembling, stunned, long drowned, guiding her on the descent, cupping her, defusing the surplus of stimulation, completing her bliss, murmuring how he'd never seen or felt or tasted anything so beautiful as her and her desire and pleasure, how he'd never thought sexual intimacy could be so sublime, his eyes heavy with awe and satisfaction.

Then he suddenly murmured, "Why didn't you tell me?"

That he'd be her first.

"It didn't occur to me." Which was the truth. She wouldn't have told him he'd be her only either. "Now I realize I should have. A man might decide to opt out if he knew, might think it an unwanted responsibility that could become some kind of obligation."

He seemed to darken and expand at her every word. "All my consideration is, has always been, and will *always* be, for you."

"Oh, Malek, I *know* that!" She hugged him, remorse compressing her heart. "What we shared, not only making love but everything we shared, every second of it, was the best thing that has ever happened to me. So I hope you're not finding more ways for it to weigh on your conscience now." Suddenly something occurred to her. "Say, would you have taken me if I'd told you?"

He gave a self-deprecating huff. "After you pointed out how you could have been lost, and *we both* wouldn't have lived first for not being together? Oh, yes, I would have." His eyes blazed with such adoration and agony-mixed contrition that her heart dropped a few beats. "But I would have initiated you so thoroughly you wouldn't have felt that much pain."

Her hands framed his face, trembling, begging his belief. "The pain was glorious, Malek—*glorious*. A searing evidence of our intimacy and an unrepeatable experience of such elemental magnitude that I probably can't describe it to you, as you never had anything comparable."

"I did," he contradicted. "Not a replica of the physical experience, but falling in love for the first time *has* been gloriously agonizing, spiritually and physically."

"Oh..." And how stupid was it that she felt jealousy crush her heart?

"You." He caught the tremor that shook her lower lip in a devouring kiss. "My first and last love."

Oh. *Oh.* He'd read her mind and insecurities again.

She surged into him, her lips and tongue mating with his in wrenching, draining kisses, the fuse of her hunger relit. Overcoming her shyness, she blindly reached for him, needing to feel his potency.

He stopped her with a look that liquefied her bones, rolled her over him, got out of bed with her wrapped around his waist.

He took her to the bathroom, and in an endless warm shower, he taught her how to satisfy her urges, how to complete her ownership of him. He was soon telling her she'd been born to drive him out of his mind, roared his surrender as she brought him to orgasm just as he brought her to another one.

They were clinging under the flow of water, moaning at the

profoundness of their intimacy, when Malek finally murmured in her mouth, "Some food is becoming an emergency, *ya roh galbi*. Then I want to share another first with you."

CHAPTER SIXTEEN

"YOU'RE TOTALLY off track," Malek murmured in Jay's ear.

"You mean it's bigger?" Jay could barely turn to gape back at him. His head was resting on her shoulder, his hard body pressed into her back, his thighs enveloping hers.

He laughed, cuddled her more securely. "If after you've been around it, you still can't guess, I'm not telling you."

She nestled into him, cast her gaze over the depression of *el waha*—the oasis that sprawled below them.

Being on top of Zeenah, Malek's mare, gave her an even higher vantage point from this, the highest elevation before the desert surrendered its dunes to the rocky terrain that heralded Jabal al Shamekh's mountainous dominion miles in the distance.

It was mind-boggling, the explosion of lush green life in the middle of the desert. Date palms and olive trees numbering in the hundreds of thousands, wild flowers and cacti, impossible in beauty and abundance, farmed fruits and vegetables, especially apricots, figs and corn, astounding in size and taste. To complete the Garden of Eden setting, beside the prerequisite horses, camels, sheep and goats, wildlife was plentiful. Malek's favorite moments were when she spotted a deer or a fox or an unknown bird and bounced up and down in delight.

Besides being breathtaking, the oasis was vast. Her last guess was fifty square miles. She gave it another go. "Seventy?"

He hugged her, laughed again. "*Ah ya malekat galbi,* I can't bear to see you burning even in curiosity. It's a hundred."

Jay shivered at the passion that permeated the lightness in his voice. He'd just called her the owner of his heart. And by now, a week after they'd first made love, a week in a heaven she hadn't dreamed existed, basking in his love, plunging deeper in their entrenching unity, she was certain she was.

She was certain of something else. This wouldn't end. He'd promised it. She knew he kept his promises.

It was unbelievable, too much to grasp, to imagine, to look forward to. But Malek was hers, like she was his, for life.

Sunset was in an hour and he'd just finished showing her the last of the oasis's wonders and its northern limits.

The oasis and its people were considered off-limits to the outside world they lived independent of. They welcomed only Malek, and whomever he invited. He'd never wanted to share the experience he treasured with another before her. He was held in such high esteem here, they even let him bring in all the laborers he needed to build his dream retreat on their land. He wouldn't tell her why.

She'd found out why in one of the feasts that had been held for them. Around a huge fire, their best storyteller had recounted the story of the knight of the desert who was riding his powerful machine, looking for solitude and communion with nature, when a sandstorm came up. He came upon a group of their young who'd foolishly tried to visit the nearest town and had got lost. They would have all died if he hadn't braved one of nature's most destructive forces, instead of blasting through it to reach safety, and if not for his healing powers.

Malek had suffered through the retelling, muttering about the hyperbole that was so integral to the region's culture. She'd only kissed him soundly, teased him about his inability to stomach people singing his praises…

"Here we are," Malek murmured in her ear.

He'd ridden back into the depths of the *waha*, brought his magnificent black mare to a halt by the *ayn*, a miniature lake of crystal-clear water enclosed within a canopy of intertwining palms where everyone, including them, fetched their drinking water, crisp and perpetually cool. The air was sweet and earthy, the temperature seemed to be calibrated for perfect comfort all year round, as he'd told her.

Malek dismounted, reached up for her, lifted her down, his effortless strength, the cherishing in his every glance and touch as she slid down his body a constant current jolting through her heart.

And she asked something that had been on her mind from day one there. "Uh, Malek, I realize the people here are nowhere as conservative as any I've seen throughout Damhoor, still, how—how did you explain my presence here?"

"I told them you are my wife." She gasped, and he pressed her harder into his embrace. "You *are* my wife, ya *janaani*. Did you think I was spouting platitudes when I said that?"

"No—no, it's just I didn't know what you meant when—when…"

"I promised forever?" he completed for her after a fierce kiss aborted her stammering distress. "I meant everything. All the way. Always. I must have it all with you. I can't live otherwise. And once we're away from here, I'll see to all the formalities and procedures. But here I married you with the oasis people, all twenty thousand of them, as witnesses. Here marriage is just this, what we have, what we did, a man and a woman being together before others, pledging to be each other's alone…" He paused at her widening eyes. "Yes, alone. Polygamy may be sanctioned in Damhoor, but here it's unheard of. Here a man weds for life. As I do you. I'll protect you, honor you, worship you all through this life. And into any other life beyond. I'd die for you."

The tears that had filled her eyes brimmed, slithered down her cheeks. "Oh, Malek, don't say that. I'd lay down my life for you to be whole and happy."

He pressed her head hard into his chest, his rasp full of remembered dread. "You already did that. Never again. No more sacrifices, *ya hayati,* of any kind." He put her away a few inches, looked down at her with possessive, entreating eyes. "Now, enough talk. I need to worship you again."

"Here?" She jerked out of his arms, looked around in alarm. She'd lost just about every inhibition with him, but she drew the line at having an audience, non-conservative or not.

Malek took her lips, began to undo the strings lacing her traditional *toab*'s front, pushing it off her shoulders, spilling her breasts into his palms, weighing and kneading them until she felt they would burst if he didn't devour them. Then he did, and she changed her mind. She *would* risk anything.

She *could* try to be quiet, and if he didn't draw out her torment like he so loved to do, maybe they could get away with it.

He returned to her lips, his tongue surging inside her, taking every intimacy she lavished. Her moans of stimulation became wild keens. They *would* get caught.

"Shall I take you now?" She could only nod her assent, her legs buckling. He held her up, smiled. "I only wanted to know if you would do anything to be with me."

"You mean this was a test?" His smile widened and she bit into his maddening lips. "Now you'd better ride us back home quickly. I have this elaborate revenge to exact on you!"

"Wouldn't you rather exact it here?"

"But you said—"

"If you think I'd ever expose you to any discomfort, you still don't realize a fraction of the depth of my love for you. We have the place to ourselves, *ya hayati*."

"What did you do?" She gaped at him. "Send twenty thousand people out on an errand?"

"I only put their wish to bestow any privilege on me to good use, to make a fantasy of mine come true. Making love to you out in the open, under the sun and moon, melding with nature.

No one will come within a mile of here till dawn. Now enough talk, I'm hungry for you again, *ya mashoogati.*"

Her *toab* snagged on her hips. He reversed his efforts, to get it over her head and she croaked, "Rip it."

His eyes widened. Then with a growl of voracity he ripped the red satin in two. She lurched and moaned to every ripping sound, relishing his frenzy, fueling it.

He could have taken his own white *toab* off in one sweep. He gave her a ferocious strip-shredding show instead. Sunshine trickled between the breeze-swaying palm crowns, an hypnotic light show accompanying his performance. Passion rose from her depths at the savage poetry of his every straining muscle. To her disappointment he was still wearing jeans underneath.

Before she could beg him to complete his show, he rushed to Zeenah, brought back a thick spread, threw it over the sand at her feet. He came down before her, buried his face in her flesh, muttered love and hunger, dragged her down, spread her on her back, eliciting more frenzy as he probed her with deft fingers.

He growled his satisfaction at her response as her slick flesh gripped his fingers. "Do you know what it does to me—to feel you like this, to have this privilege, this freedom? Do you know what it means to me that you let me, that you want me, that you're mine?"

Sensation rocketed, more at the maelstrom of emotions and passions fueling his words than at his expert pleasuring. She screamed, opened herself fully to him, now willing to accept pleasure any way he gave it, knowing he craved her surrender, her pleasure. She'd always give him all he wanted.

His tongue thrust inside her mouth to the rhythm of his invading fingers, while his thumb ground her bud in escalating circles. He swallowed every whimper of agonized pleasure, every tremulous word detailing it, every tear at its overpowering effect, until she shuddered in his arms.

She collapsed. Totally nerveless and sated. For about two

minutes. Then she was kneading his masculinity through his jeans, and he rasped, "Release me."

She undid the zipper with shaking hands. Her mouth watered as he sprang heavy and throbbing into her hands. He groaned in a bass voice that shook her insides, spilled magma from her core.

"Play with me, *ya galbi*. Own me. I'm yours."

"And do you know what hearing you say that means to me?" she groaned back, her hand nowhere near closing around his girth, again stunned that her hunger was so vast it accommodated so much demand. "This, you, are literally to die for, *ya habibi*."

He snatched her in his arms, groaning with revisited anguish. "To *live* for. Live for me, be happy with me, be mine and let me be yours, Janaan."

He roared as her hands traveled up and down his silken steel shaft, pumping his mind-blowing potency in delight. Then she slithered down his body, tasted him all the way down to his hot, smooth crown. His scent, taste and texture made her whimper with need for all of him. She opened her mouth and took all she could of him inside. Growling his ecstasy, he thrust his hips to her suckling rhythm.

Suddenly, his hand in her hair stopped her. Then she was beneath him, impaled, complete, the pleasure of his occupation insupportable.

"Ma'boodati," he ranted in her mouth, driving deeper and deeper into her. "*Hayati elek*—my life is yours, *ya habibati*..."

Answering pledges spilled from her until she felt the pulse of pleasure tighten, the heat focused in her loins desperate for one more stoke to burst into the fire that would consume her. He gave her just what she needed for her world to implode, fed her convulsions, slamming her into the soft sand, pumping her to the last abrading twitches of fulfillment.

Then he surrendered to his own climax, and the sight of him, the sound of him reaching completion inside her, the feel of his seed jetting his passion into her, filling her to overflowing, had her in the throes of another orgasm until she was weeping, unable to bear the stimulation.

Still buried inside her, he withdrew to view her tear-drenched face. His eyes promised more, all the time, languid and proprietorial, with that added imperious gleam of his Middle Eastern blood. Royal blood to boot.

Carrying her nerveless body, he prowled to Bir Al-Shefa, the warm sulfur spring outside the grove where he'd soaked her so many times, completing her healing. Its waters had done wonders. It was aptly named the well of healing.

He stepped into the water, waded in until he was knee deep, took her down into it, laid her between his thighs, her back to his front, sat supporting her as she half floated.

He moved water over her satiated body, massaging her with it, and she hummed to the bliss reverberating in her bones, in her blood.

She would have taken this if he'd only promised this week. She would have lived on the memories forever. But this was forever. It was so unbelievable she woke up suffocating, believing he'd vanished, had never been hers, that it had all been a delusion. She had to touch him to assure herself he was really there, had to remind herself that he'd promised.

Her heart suddenly started hammering. Felt as if it would ram out of her chest. As if she was having a panic attack. She'd never had one. God—what was wrong with her?

Oblivious to her condition, Malek sighed in contentment, whispered, "*Aashagek.*"

Aasahagek. Mashoogati. The verb and adjective of *esh'g*, a concept with no equivalent in English. Far more selfless and intense than love, too carnal for adoration, and as reverent as worship and as impossible to shake. It fit perfectly what she felt for him.

She struggled to bring the quaking that was threatening to break to the surface under control, turned her face into his cushioning chest and whispered back, "*Wa ana aashagak.*"

Then they heard it. The single-tone ring of his cellphone. Zeenah. She'd trotted after them, bringing it to him.

Malek exhaled a rough breath. "No way am I answering that."

The quaking broke free. She shook, struggled to sit up.

"It could be important."

"I called the palace before lunch," he muttered, his voice thick with displeasure. "Surely the kingdom can spare me longer than six hours at a time."

"Please, Malek, answer it."

The moon was blazing now. He could no doubt see her twisted face, her body now shaking in earnest.

He rose out of the water, swooped down, half carried her. "*Ma beeki, ya habibati?* What's wrong?"

"Noth-nothing." Her teeth clattered with a surge of agitation, foreboding nearly strangling her by now. "Just—just…"

He rushed her back to Zeenah, dried her, dressed her in an extra *toab* of his, his eyes growing more anxious as he took in her deteriorating state. The phone didn't stop ringing.

Just to end its disconcerting effect on her, he snatched it out of his backpack, barked into it, *"Aish betreed ya Saeed?"*

Jay heard the rush of agitated speech on the other end. Stopped breathing as Malek lurched under the barrage, froze.

An eternity later, he raised blank eyes to her. She almost fell to her knee with the impact of dread.

Then dread became reality, rasped on a voice that had turned darker than the desert's moonless nights.

"My father is dead."

Long live the king boomed in her head.

CHAPTER SEVENTEEN

THE NEXT TWO weeks were a nightmare.

Seeing Malek's grief deepening as the knowledge of his father's death and that he was the last of his family, the king now, was her first real glimpse into hell. She stood helplessly by as all through the funeral and the initial days of mourning, matters of state deluged Malek, keeping him from her. But he swore it was her nearness that made him able to bear it all, begged her to stay near. He needed her.

It was all she lived for, to be there for him when he came back to her, seeking solace.

She stayed in his residence, a secluded building connected to the palace by a grand passageway, waiting for him to come to her, exhausted and anguished, surrender it all in her arms for short hours before rising to continue dealing with the demands of a kingdom that was suddenly in turmoil.

She asked what was happening. He only said not to worry. He was handling everything. His answer, made with a guarded eye and leaden voice, made her worry rise to insurmountable levels.

He hadn't come back to her at all last night. He'd even turned off his cellphone.

She was just about to lose her mind with a thousand nightmares when she heard his convoy arriving at the palace.

She exploded out of their quarters. She had to beg him to include her, let her help, in any way.

She rushed out into the spacious corridors leading to his stateroom, saw nothing of the impossible grandeur of her surroundings. The guards stood at attention as she approached, opened the door of the antechamber with all the ceremony they showed Malek. She went in, heard Malek's raised voice through the ajar door of the stateroom—and froze.

He sounded furious, cornered. *Oh, God—what was wrong?*

"So you will really risk a civil war for your bastard, half-breed whore?" another man's voice demanded in Arabic.

A sudden explosion of violence answered him. The muffled sound of an unstoppable force hitting flesh and bones, the sound of a heavy body crashing to the ground.

Deathly silence fell, interrupted only by the heavy breathing of those inside with Malek. She'd stopped breathing.

Then Malek's voice broke out, drenching her in shivers at its murderous coldness. "I didn't kill you, Zayd, because I know you're a fool. But being one will not grant you a second chance. As long as I live, you're never to enter this palace again, and you're relieved of your position, which demands wisdom and control and diplomacy, everything you so grossly lack. And if you ever repeat your opinion of Janaan again, in any form, anywhere, I will have you tried, and convicted, for defamation. You know the sentence."

A long silence followed, punctuated with what she knew was the struck man's efforts to pull himself up to his feet.

Then Malek spoke again, and she wondered if they all fell to their knees as she wanted to. "Janaan is the reason you have a king today. You should pray in thanks for her."

Another voice, precise and tranquil with age and wisdom, rose. "Zayd was criminally slanderous. You were merciful in your decrees. But as your late father's advisor, I urge you to consider our solution. If your beloved is the matchless woman you paint her, she'll appreciate the magnitude of your duties, will help you carry them out. And then she will be honored, given a life of untold luxury. What woman can dream of more than that?"

Malek let out an ugly laugh. "Offering Janaan luxury is like offering a perfect falcon extra wings. And how will I honor her without proclaiming her mine to the world?"

Jay couldn't hear more. Shouldn't have heard it at all, hadn't meant to hear it. She just couldn't move.

She *had* to.

She forced her legs to move but she stumbled, bumped into a pillar with an urn on top of it. The crash sent her collapsing on the nearest divan, brought men rushing in from every direction. She only saw Malek, saw how his face contorted the moment he saw her.

With one fierce order, he cleared the room. Then, wordlessly, he scooped her up in his arms, took her to the stateroom, closed the door securely behind them. He lowered her onto another divan, came down on his knees before her, clutching her hands, his face clenched in agitation and entreaty.

Before he could say anything, she rasped out weakly, "Your problems—the uproar in the kingdom—they're all over me, aren't they?"

"No, no." He rose, kissed her all over her face. "I promised I'll take care of it, and I will."

She shook her head and he brought an urgent hand to her face. A cry of horror tore out of her. She groped for his hand, slid shaking fingers over his swollen, discolored knuckles.

His irreplaceable hands, his surgeon's miraculous tools, injured in her defense. He could have impaired them forever. What more injuries and losses must he endure on her account?

"What I would give for you not to have heard that, *ya habibati*." He kissed her hand, a knuckle at a time.

"I didn't mean to, but I did, and I need you to please tell me the rest."

For a long moment he struggled with loathing to inflict more on her. Then he finally exhaled, heavy and resigned.

"There's no dispute that the house of Munsoor Aal-Hamdaan,

my great-grandfather, is the rightful one. But there are other branches of the Aal-Hamdaan family, as well as ancient tribes who have always had a part of the rule through marriage into Munsoor's line. I told the elders of the candidate houses that I won't have sons of their blood, that when I'm dead they should decide who will rule after me."

"Th-that has only made the dispute over who will rule after you start right now, threatening a civil war." He acknowledged the accuracy of her conclusion with a curt nod, his color now deep copper. "What is the solution?"

He gritted his teeth. "They suggest I first take a wife the kingdom will accept, then, as our religion permits in extreme conditions, to invoke my right to take you as my second wife."

"And this is the only way, isn't it?"

This was a rhetorical question. He still answered it, vehement, final. "No, it isn't. I haven't accepted their solution. And I won't. I will find another way."

Suddenly he crushed her in his arms. "I *will* find a way—just give me more time. *La t'seebeeni ya rohi*—don't leave me, don't even think it. I can see you, *feel* you thinking it." He crushed her harder into him, his hand burying her face in his neck, every convulsion of his Adam's apple, every break in his ragged voice a shock wave of misery and desperation. Her heart bled, tears escaped down her face. He shook her, frantic to drag her back to him, to keep her there. "Promise me you won't leave me. Give me your pledge, Janaan."

She only nodded, buried her face in his neck again.

A harsh exhalation spilled from his lips, relief made audible, before he tilted her face up, poured love and dependence over her. "*Ashkorek, ya mashoogati*—thank you. I will never let you down."

"I will never do what you're asking, *ya doctorah*!"

"You *must*, Saeed." Jay heard the manic edge lacing her shrill voice. She was going crazy with fear that he'd refuse her. Run to Malek. That she wouldn't be able to run away. "You must help me get out of Damhoor."

"But why?" Saeed's desert-hardened face for once reflected his emotions. Confusion, agitation. Disappointment.

"Because my presence is blinding Malek to the fact that he has far more important things than me to worry about—a whole nation's peace and future."

Saeed obsidian eyes only hardened. "King Malek is convinced that he has your pledge to remain by his side until he reaches a solution that will allow him to take you, and only you, as his wife. You want to break your pledge?"

"I *must.*" It was a cry so shrill it made him wince. She panted, continued, her voice wobbling. "There is no solution and he knows it. But right now he's willing to risk anything to keep his pledge to me. I can't let him do this to Damhoor, to himself. Without me in the picture, he'll be the most powerful, most benevolent king who ever lived. With me he'll be a ruler at war with his own country, finding no peace, ending up with strife on his conscience, even blood on his hands, and I'm—I'm not w-worth that, n-nothing is…"

She wept. Until she felt she'd dissolve and solve everyone's problems. Saeed watched her break down in utter helplessness.

A long time later, still quaking, she struggled to talk through the hacking sobs. "By leaving I'll remove the one reason this prosperous land might find itself in the throes of a civil war—like those tearing so many neighboring nations apart."

Saeed shook his salt-and-pepper head. "King Malek said he'll find a way. And he will. Don't you have faith in him?"

"I have every faith in him," she cried. "But he's not thinking clearly now. Malek...his fortitude staggers me but even he has limits and he's taken more blows in the last year than anyone should endure in ten lifetimes. Majd, his father, finding himself crowned king, being forced to relinquish his vocation, his freedom. And he'd already demanded too much of himself, drawing on his reserves constantly, pouring himself into his work. I hoped to be his biggest support but I'm now his greatest burden and I'll remain that and I can't…"

"*You* can't?" Saeed barked. "What about King Malek? I thought no man could love a woman like I loved my late wife. But his love for you makes what drove me to despair for years, what makes me unable to feel anything for another woman ever again, seem like nothing. Your desertion will kill him!"

"No!" The paroxysm drove her to her knees, raining tears on the very ground Malek walked on. *"Please*—don't. I'm leaving so he can *live*, be in peace, be happy—eventually. He'll forget me. It'll be difficult at first, but time and distance will—"

"*Nothing* will make him forget." Saeed's harsh growl interrupted her torn words. "King Malek was born on my hands, as we say here. I never knew anyone more steadfast. He's fastidious with his trust but, once won, his trust is for life, he's wary to commit, but once he commits only death can make him break his commitments. With you he's compounded total trust and commitment with what he'll never give another woman—love."

"Don't—I can't take this…" she almost screamed. "If I stay, and all hell breaks loose, he'll end up hating me. Or he'll be forced to take a wife to stem the conflicts and I—I…"

"You're really thinking of yourself here, aren't you?" Saeed lashed out. "You're afraid he'll come to hate you, so you want to save yourself possible future discomfort by breaking his heart now. You can't bear the idea of sharing him with another woman even for the cause you claim to find so much bigger than yourself because you're afraid he'll find you wanting in contrast to his imposed wife. You want to save yourself the humiliation of a comparison you believe you'll lose."

His words fell on her like scythes. But it wasn't their mercilessness that she felt— it was the razor sharpness of the images they evoked.

Malek, in a royal ceremony, god-like, exchanging vows with

the woman he'd settle on to appease his kingdom. Malek, running to her to make good on his pledge.

Then time passed and the pressure for an heir grew, and he went to his first wife, a woman to fit a king, raised from birth to be a queen, favored by all, the instrument of peace and prosperity, his equal in beauty and refinement, sharing his background and culture, versed in all the nuances Jay could never learn, and in the arts of seducing and servicing her man.

And he joined his body to hers, took his pleasure inside her, spilled his seed and came to covet her, even love her, with the bond of children cementing her hold over him.

While Jay became the woman he looked on in disappointment and confusion, wondering how he'd once contemplated risking so much for her, concluding that his emotional turmoil at the time and the ordeals they'd shared had deluded him, had coated her blandness with magic, a magic that drained away with each layer of stability his new family brought to his life, every encounter of true passion he shared with his rightful wife.

But though he no longer felt anything for her but pity for her dependence, regret for his unintentional exploitation, even revulsion for her continued hunger, he'd show her mercy.

And she finally understood what her mother had suffered. How she'd come to end her own life.

Not that she ever would. But she felt them now. The depths of desperation that could make a slow, painful death a release.

She rose to suddenly steady feet, her voice unwavering as she heard herself say, "You're right."

Saeed jerked as if she'd slapped him. He'd been goading her to rage against his accusations, to prove their falseness by staying near his master and forgetting her moment of weakness.

For a long moment he searched her now dry eyes. She knew he'd find nothing there. He'd shown her the future and everything she was had died just getting a glimpse at it.

"I always believed my master's judgment unerring," he finally drawled. "His belief in your worth formed a great part of my regard for you. But if you won't lay down your life for a man of his greatness, let alone weather some hardships and uncertainties, it seems both of us have been wrong this time."

It was another attempt to rouse her to self-defense. It had no effect. Neither did the contemptuous if still pleading accusation in his eyes.

So this was what her mother had sought in death. The anesthesia. The cessation. The nothingness.

She wiped the last of the wetness from her cheeks. "Then you should be glad that your master will be rid of such a fickle weakling so unfit of his passion and faith. Will you help me get out of Damhoor now? He assigned a dozen of his best men to my protection and service now he's scared for my safety. I won't be able to go anywhere without him knowing about it. And as he's still under the spell of his misguided affections, he'll come after me."

Saeed still hesitated, unable to shake his own affection and faith that easily. Any minute now he'd conclude she was in the grip of understandable turmoil, would do her the merciful courtesy of forgetting her temporary lapse. Then she'd be trapped here. She'd end up destroying Malek, and Damhoor.

She lashed out in a last desperate attempt with the most vicious thing she could think of. "If you don't help me out of here, I'll call the American embassy and accuse Malek of holding me here against my will."

And if she still had a life, she would have feared for it at that moment.

As it was, the flare of murderous fury in Saeed's eyes only told her she'd be out of there before she knew what hit her.

She'd won.

And she'd lost. Everything.

CHAPTER EIGHTEEN

"I'M LOSING HER!" Jay shouted at her scrabbling team in the chaotic ER as she checked their car-crash casualty's plummeting vitals. She turned to one of her three nurses. "Heather, get me an echocardiogram. Then I'm going for a pericardiocentesis under echocardiographic guidance."

Mrs. Dobbs had all signs of cardiac tamponade. Engorged neck veins, absent heart sounds, plummeting blood pressure not responsive to treatment. Blood was pumping out of a tear in one of the heart's chambers, filling the pericardium, compressing the ventricles to a standstill.

Jay had to introduce a needle through the chest, enter the pericardial sac and drain all she could of the blood.

"Sally, 20-gauge cardiac needle," Jay ordered. "Fifty-mil syringe. Josh, ready the defibrillator. Then elevate bed to 45 degrees."

She snatched the echocardiogram from Heather, found the tamponade. Massive. Rapidly fatal if left to accumulate further.

She dragged the echocardiogram machine nearer, looked at the images on the monitor, advanced the needle towards the shoulder, injected air. She detected the bubbles on the monitor within the pericardial sac. She was in!

She aspirated and blood gushed, filling the syringe.

After a drastic improvement in blood pressure and pulse,

blood re-accumulated, and they aspirated again. On the fourth aspiration the woman fibrillated.

She snatched the charged defibrillator from Josh, shouted, "Clear."

The woman responded with the first jolt, sinus rhythm resuming. But in minutes she fibrillated again.

After the second defibrillation, Jay knew what had to do done. Something she'd only done once. The patient had died then.

"She needs an emergency thoracotomy."

It was Jay's heart that stopped this time. And wouldn't start again.

It couldn't be. It couldn't. Not here. Not him.

Malek.

She swung around, breathless, mindless, found him a foot behind her, his eyes flaring amber even in the ER's fluorescent light.

Malek. Her soul made flesh, made man, the man who'd once been hers, the soul she'd resigned herself to existing without.

His hand took her arm and she almost wailed with the wrench of longing.

"Let's do this," he whispered as he snapped on gloves, turned to the nurses who were gaping at him, knowing they were in the presence of a higher medical authority. "We'll need a scalpel with a 10 blade, curved scissors, rib spreader, Gigli saw. And a full hemostatic set."

Everyone turned to Jay, asking her permission to follow this unknown person's orders. Jay only nodded, not knowing what she was nodding for, and stared up at him. *Malek, Malek, Malek, here, here, here* were the only things she heard, saw, knew. He pressed her arm again and it was only her paralysis that stopped her from launching herself into his arms.

"I'm really here, so make use of me, hmm?" He gave her a strange smile, tight and unnatural then turned to the nurses. "Prep the field." He looked down at her. "Shall I do it?"

She nodded again, and he immediately made an incision from

the sternum to the mid-axillary line then murmured, "Rib spreader." She automatically handed it to him. He inserted it between the ribs, opened them. "Gigli saw." She handed it to him too. He divided the sternum, moved the rib spreader to the midline. He made a small incision in the pericardium then tore it open with a finger, evacuating blood and clots.

The sight of the cardiac wounds oozing blood brought her out of her stupor. She jumped forward, provided hemorrhage control to the largest one with direct finger pressure while he sutured lesser wounds. In under two minutes he'd performed a meticulous repair of two wounds in the ascending aorta and one in the left atrium. And the woman arrested again.

"You do internal cardiac massage," he murmured. "Your hands are the perfect size for it."

She nodded, did a two-handed technique for a better cardiac output and to avoid the risk of cardiac perforation. The heart restarted, and this time didn't stop again.

It was a blur as they concluded the procedure.

As orderlies took their patient to IC, all she wanted to do was collapse. To weep her heart out at the shock and disbelief of his sudden reappearance.

Malek, here in Seattle, after six months of self-imposed exile in the hell of a life without him, working with her like they'd done before, more needed than her hands and eyes, saving the patient she would have lost on her own or with lesser help.

She staggered to the doctors' room, not looking back, praying he was a figment of her tortured imagination. Once inside, hands grabbed her shoulders. They were his.

He turned her, and she almost doubled over at the sight of the silver that had invaded his temples, at the reflection of her own unremitting longing on his haggard face.

She'd give anything to always see him whole and happy, not with the signs of aging anguish robbing his hair of its raven vividness, his eyes and face of their indomitable vitality.

Those signs said he was real. Real. And he was there to plunge himself into more torment, unable to let her go, as she hadn't been able to let him go.

But nothing had changed, as he'd once told her before she'd done him the ultimate injury and dragged him deeper into their addiction. Yet no one but her paid the price of hers. A whole country paid for his. She didn't matter. He did.

And she had to help him let go.

Mustering the last of her will, she stepped out of his almost-embrace, feigned lightness as she said, "This is one hell of a surprise, Malek. And one hell of a favor. I would have lost Mrs. Dobbs without your help."

He only nodded, his eyes darkening, wary, watching her every breath, as if he was trying to read her thoughts and feelings.

She went to the dressing room, put on her summer coat. Her personal thermostat had been shot to hell of late. She was freezing now.

She came out, found him standing in the same spot where she'd left him, a stoop to his wide shoulders, and her heart almost knocked her off her feet. She'd seen him exhausted, agitated, uncertain, but seeing him defeated, lost…

Oh, Malek, my love, not on my account, I beg you.

Determined more than ever to end this, to send him back to his life, and out of hers, forever this time, she forced a brittle smile. "So how did you find me?"

"You're asking because you hoped I wouldn't, right?" This was said with such pain she almost fell to her knees to beg his forgiveness. "You hid well. It took my intelligence machine, aided by the American one, all this time to find you."

She attempted a smile. "Hope the CIA and FBI didn't think you wanted me for some crime committed on Damhoorian soil."

His only answer was a grimace before he bent his head, examined his feet in utter bleakness for a moment.

Then he straightened, like someone bracing himself for a fatal blow. "I guess as you didn't want me to find you, you're not exactly happy I'm here." He stopped, a vulnerability she'd never seen entering his eyes, his posture, as if he was begging her to contradict him. She managed not to at the price of years off her life. He went on, his jaw muscles working, the rest of his face barely under control, "Happy or not, I don't think it's too much to ask to talk. If you'll, please, come with me, where we can be alone."

Alone. Didn't he know she'd always remain so without him? He should never know. But to be alone with him again…

The decision overtook her, left her lips. "OK."

His tension deflated as if with a gut punch. Then he strode towards her, his intention to take her in his arms explicit in every ravenous line and move. She pretended to spin around to fetch her bag. She straightened to find him two steps away, bewilderment and hurt coming off of him in waves.

And she made a second mistake. "Would you like to come to my place?"

He staggered a step backward, confusion twisting his beloved face. Then determination hardened it and he took her arm, gripped it harder than necessary as he guided her out of the hospital, as if afraid she'd dissolve if he loosened his hold.

People turned to gape at him. Not only was he the most magnificent male on earth, they must recognize him, too, must be wondering what a king was doing there, and with her to boot.

Outside, the limo awaiting them wasn't a diplomatic one. Saeed was the driver. She met his eyes as he opened the door for them, saw that the accusation and the fury of their last encounter had turned into something akin to hatred.

She faltered. "Maybe this isn't a good idea after all…"

Malek's hand tightened. "No, Janaan. You're not running out on me again. Not before we talk. Get in, please."

He'd said "please", but she knew he'd haul her over his shoulder all the way to her condo if she refused. She got in.

She kept her eyes averted, looking into nothingness as Seattle zoomed by.

She didn't need to give her address. He already knew it. She wondered how much more he knew. Wondered what would happen once they were alone.

Nothing, she railed at herself. Nothing would happen, then he'd be the one to walk out on her this time. This time forever.

In thirty minutes he was taking her key from her, unlocking her door and pushing it open for her.

She walked into her utilitarian space on rigid, numb legs and her bag dropped out of her nerveless fingers. It fell on the couch she passed by, didn't betray her collapsing condition.

She leaned on the first wall she reached, asked with forced brightness, "Would you like something to drink?"

"I would like you to stop behaving as if we're strangers," he grated, waited for a reaction. When there was none, he prowled into her reception area, shrinking it, making everything look drab and insignificant in comparison, her neat place, herself—life. Then his gaze suddenly slammed into her, pinned her to the wall like a butterfly on a board.

Then he finally rasped, "Did you see the ceremony?"

And Jay felt her world ending all over again.

She'd been waiting for the guillotine blade to fall, but it still hacked her to pieces when it did. She'd been avoiding all media—and people—like the plague. Anyone who'd known she'd been to Damhoor had wanted to relate news of the country and its exciting new hunk of a king. She'd shut herself out, unable to bear hearing any mention of him or his country.

And here he was, forcing the news on her.

So he'd had a ceremony. Had chosen a wife. The wife considered suitable, the wife he'd now take to bed, or might have already taken to bed, the one who'd bear him heirs, or might already be bearing the first of many.

But it seemed his new wife's charms hadn't worked yet. Or

was he not giving the woman a chance, because he was still pining for *her*? Or maybe he was there to appease his honor, fulfill his pledge, offer her the best he could provide, a position as his second wife. And he was waiting for an answer.

She could only give an uncoordinated shrug that could be read as yes or no, as if it didn't matter to her which.

Malek watched Jan with a heart that had shriveled to a husk since the moment he'd discovered her disappearance. He'd exploded in rages, mobilized all the kingdom's resources in searches and investigations, had even threatened all the tribes with retribution if anyone had had a hand in her disappearance.

It had been then that Saeed had confessed, had tried to convince him the Janaan he loved didn't exist, that the real woman had shown her true colors at the first hurdle. The accusations hadn't even registered, had only incensed him into being ruthless in his punishment of Saeed.

Then he'd swept the earth looking for her.

But all through the soul-gnawing, mind-eroding desperation; dread, fury, and longing, he'd had no doubt. Not a shadow of one. His self-sacrificing Janaan loved him with all her soul, had left him thinking she was doing what was best for him and Damhoor.

Then she'd looked at him with cool, distant eyes, treated him as if they didn't mean life and beyond to each other, and his world had smashed around him. He'd never known such helplessness, such fear, such defeat.

Could it have been true? She'd left him because she didn't love him enough? Didn't love him at all?

Then he'd asked if she'd seen the ceremony. And she'd only shrugged. *Ya Ruhmaan*—she didn't care?

What would he do if she didn't? He could no longer make a rational thought without her being the main pillar in his mind, could no longer exist if she wasn't at the core of his reasons and goals.

Then everything evaporated from his mind. She was taking off her coat and—and he couldn't believe he hadn't noticed before.

She was pregnant!

His incomparable Janaan, carrying a child! *His child.*

The only child he wanted. The child he'd hoped they'd been making each time they'd made love. He'd rejoiced when she hadn't brought up the matter of protection. The meticulous doctor would have insisted on it if it hadn't been her ultimate method of showing him she'd wanted his seed to take root inside her, had trusted him with her body, her future and that of her child's. *Their* child.

Then mortification rose in a black tide.

Had she suspected it when she'd left him? Was that why she had? She'd sacrificed herself for what she believed was the best for him, intending to go through pregnancy, childbirth and his child's upbringing without his love and support?

No more. Never again. He'd be her support and succor for every moment from now on. The next baby, he'd be there from the first moment, for every second after that till his last breath.

He hadn't felt himself move, but he was all around her, cascading passion and protection and tears of gratitude and pride over her down to where his child was growing healthy and strong inside her.

But she was pushing him away, frantic, feeble fingers trying to terminate his homage, her sobs drowning his ragged rasps. "Don't, Malek. I'm—I'm four months pregnant…"

It didn't make sense at first. Then the words mushroomed in his mind like a nuclear detonation. Four months.

Four.

His hands convulsed in her flesh, an instinctive spasm, warding off the horror, the devastation, the fatal blow.

He raised his eyes to hers, begging for a renunciation, a stay of execution of all his hopes and dreams, his faith, but found nothing but tears. Of guilt? Of pity?

A white-hot vice crushed his chest.

He willed it to complete the job, still its beating.

It didn't. *Why?* So he'd live with it?

He couldn't! He couldn't live at all.

Janaan's child wasn't his.

She'd forgotten him in days—*days*. Had craved another, had opened her body to his invasion, taken his seed, wanting *it* to bear fruit not *his*.

He heard something crackling, congealing with agony and madness, a butchered maniac ranting his last breaths away.

"All for nothing. All the certainty, the *invincibility* in her—for worse than nothing. For an illusion. Not mine—not mine…"

Jay reeled as Malek fragmented before her eyes.

But this isn't what I meant to do, she wanted to scream.

She'd die to never see him in pain.

She flew after him, threw herself at his feet. He staggered, looked down at her with the eyes of a man in the process of losing his coherence. And she begged.

"Forgive me, Malek, please, please—forgive me. I lied, lied—only to set you free. I thought you'd just despise me, walk away, be free of me. I swear I never dreamed it would hurt you this much. My baby is yours, Malek, as I am, as I will always be. I just want you strong and in peace—please, Malek, please…"

The look in his eyes changed to the wild one of someone way past his limit, the tears she'd never thought to see pouring from them, and she panicked, her words colliding with each other in her fright.

"You said I had to have a family, and now I do, Malek—I do! Your child will be all the family I need. You shouldn't worry about me, about us. I'm a good provider and I'll be a good mother. I am nothing like my mother—please, please, never worry on that account. And if you want and find it possible to participate in your child's life in any way, you can. You can do anything you want or see fit to. Anything at all."

Malek looked down at Janaan, his salvation and destruction, demolished twice over. With the devastation of her sacrifice, after the devastation of her attempt to drive him away.

He fell to his knees before her, shaken to his foundations that she was all he'd believed and more, that he'd never be able to love her hard or long enough, never have enough, never.

"*Hada kateer—kateer.* This is too much..." he reiterated as it all merged into a dream sequence, after the harrowing plunge into the nightmare of annihilation, and she was cleaved to him, her tears mingling with his, her passion a chain reaction with his, melting their barriers, their flesh together.

Then he went home, plunged inside her, drove in a ferocious rhythm, weeping at the poignancy of union, of reunion, of souls and bodies sundered and now remade into one.

At the peak he drew away to watch her, his Janaan, his heart and mind and soul in name and reality, taking her fill of him, at the mercy of the pleasure he inundated her with, magnanimous with her captivation of him, with her surrender.

Only when she started tumbling down the vortex of pleasure, crying out her love, convulsing around him, wrenching his release from his every cell, he joined her, spilled his seed, branded her as his forever, only sorry that he couldn't give her another child right now.

Then there was peace. For the first true time in his life.

Their union had started with their first eye melding, but this was the beginning of an inseparable life together.

He lay curved around her, his lips traveling over her neck and shoulders, her hand luxuriating in the evidence of his love growing inside her, pride blazing through him, spilling on words of worship, pledges of forever.

Her quivering finally stopped, her caresses, too. He growled with deprivation, took her hands back to his body, urged them to resume their ownership. She resisted him. A black spot began to grow in the perfection again. He drew himself up on one elbow.

"Malek—this was a lapse..."

His heart contracted at her choking statement.

He no longer understood anything. There was no logic to grasp at here. He gathered her tighter to his body. "The most powerful intimacy we've ever shared, a *lapse*?"

She was panting, peach-flushed, her eyes turquoise in the bedside light, slumberous with the drug of pleasure, bleak with the admission of defeat. "Yes—one I'll keep making if you don't leave me alone. I know what you came to offer me, and I can't accept. So, please, leave me alone, Malek, please..."

The black spot was expanding, about to consume his world again. "You're having my child, you say you're mine forever, you just made soul-shattering love with me, but you won't marry me? Is this what you're saying? What is this? Pregnancy hormones?"

She turned her face into the pillow, bit her lip to stop its trembling. "I'm trying not to intrude in your life, take you from your duties and your wife. I can't be the other woman in your life. It will destroy me as it destroyed my mother." She turned a tear-drenched face of overpowering beauty and poignancy to him. "If you stay away long enough, we may be able to grow a thick scab over the wound to live with it, but if you keep reopening the wound, letting the hunger bleed out, it will keep eating at us until nothing is left. I want to have your baby, Malek, I want to be whole and strong and nurturing. Please, my love, help me retain my sanity, don't keep reminding me how much I'm losing, how much I can't have."

Malek reeled, everything inside his head in chaos. "What are you talking about? What duties? What wife? You said—at least *implied*—that you'd seen the ceremony! The ceremony where I abdicated and handed the crown to my cousin!"

* * *

Jay was convinced now. This was all a psychotic breakdown.

She couldn't have heard Malek correctly.

"*Abdicated?*" She heard the explosive word, realized it had just erupted from her lips. "I thought you meant a marriage ceremony and… *Abdicated!* God—how? *Why?* How *could* you?"

The distressed bewilderment in his eyes slowly gave way to amusement. Then suddenly he threw his head back and laughed. Peal after peal of cruelly masculine merriment that was all him.

Her inarticulate cry of chagrin and impatience brought a reluctant end to his fit.

He still chuckled as he trailed a hand heavy with possession over her ripeness. "*Ahen ya habibat galbi.* If you only saw what I see now, you'd excuse me if I made love to you again now and explained later." At her warning growl he took his hand off her, held it up. "All right. As for how, not at all easily, and that was what kept me the past six months from tearing the world apart with my own hands to find you. I had to make everyone agree to my decision, to agree on who best to replace me. They were so desperate for me to remain on the throne they even agreed to let me take you as my wife."

Would she have any reason left when he was through with her?

"They agreed that you can marry me and remain king?" she paraphrased slowly, as if to make sure she hadn't imagined hearing it. Then she shouted, *"So why did you abdicate?"*

He smiled in indulgence at her distraught reaction. "Simply because I would have married you, then barely seen you, as duties deluged me in a totally different sphere from the one you move in as a doctor. They tried to convince me I could still be a doctor, work with you, but I realistically know I can't be both a hands-on doctor and a king, and I had to choose. Not only you as my life-mate, but the kind of life we'll lead together.

"I chose the only life where we'll be happy, together and fulfilled. What I have to offer the world of medicine and healthcare is something no one else can. My cousin is a better statesman than I am. It was decreed that he won't make pivotal decisions without my approval, that I'll still have massive sway in the kingdom. And I plan to use that power, with you, to be the driving force behind advancement and moderation.

"We'll be together, living each day to the full in each other's nearness and nurturing, doing what we do best, being healers. Though we may have to take it a bit easier when each of our children is too young. I hope to have one more."

And she wept. Felt like she'd dissolve.

What he was saying, what he'd done was so huge it left her shocked, mute, awed, humbled, elated. Oppressed.

She launched herself at him, sobbed the excess of emotions into his chest. "How did I ever deserve all that? How *can* I ever deserve that?"

"Without the least effort," he insisted, all pride and indulgence. "Just being yourself, the woman who enslaved me with your selflessness and courage and generosity from the first moment. The woman who owns me by right of saving my life, by right of giving me my first real taste of what life means. My life started for real after we met. I only ever knew every heart-rending emotion with you and on your account. And you are the only one who shares my vision, my drive, my soul. Together we'll be an unstoppable force for good." He hugged her fiercely. "It's a relief you're giving me a child, *ya rohi.* I hope a daughter, who can act as a safety valve for the dangerous accumulation of love I have for you." He pinched her cheek softly. "I wouldn't want to exhaust you."

Stumbling deeper in stunned, humble ecstasy, drowning, soaring with so many things that she'd need her lifetime to fully register and savor them, Jay hugged him, took his lips.

"Our child will have to be satisfied with a separate reservoir of love," she said, her voice ragged, drenched in tears and smiles. "My love for you is all yours. As for exhausting me, no way. In fact, I'm so well rested it constitutes an emergency. You should do something about it."

And he did. How he did.

After one more rocketing journey to their private place in heaven, melted with pleasure and security in his arms, she mumbled, "I'll have to disappoint you on one account. Your firstborn will regretfully be the wrong gender. And *that* sounds so weird now I said it out loud. I thought you desert knights valued male firstborns above all things."

He winced. "Not this desert knight. I was really hoping our first foray into parenthood wouldn't involve one of those unmanageable male Aal Hamdaans. The females, like my aunts, are simply exquisite." He suddenly hugged her exuberantly. "You'd better start practicing how to give birth to Damhoor's future king."

She gaped at him. "Wha—?"

"*Aih*, they let me abdicate only with the promise that my firstborn son would be king, that my cousin would act as regent until he came of age. They want the line of Munsoor Aal Hamdaan to be reinstated on the throne as soon as possible."

And she spluttered, unable to deal with yet another dizzying, devastating development. He brought an end to her distress in another searing kiss.

"I promise to teach you everything about raising a king." He stopped, rose on his outstretched arms to look down on her nakedness as she lay half-fainting with pleasure and shock. "But what am I saying? You already know all you need to know. You've already tamed and enslaved one, made him wish to be only king of your heart."

She put him straight. "You are king of my *life*, and beyond." Pride and joy flared in his eyes. And for some reason she thought this the right time to tell him another thing. "And I want to train to be a surgeon."

His golden eyes sparkled down on her with pride, becoming blinding. "So you're going to be a full-time lover, wife, mother to a king, doctor, but you want more?"

"Yes. This is the only way I can fully share with you all the responsibilities and experiences in our work."

He closed his eyes, as if in pain. "*Ya Ullah*, so there is more. More awe, more gratitude, more love. Always will be, with you." He took her lips in a pledging kiss, withdrew. "You can be anything you want to be. You can have anything in the world. You can have the very world, *ya janaani*."

She surged up, kissed him all over his face. "I already have it. I have you."

His eyes singed her down to her soul, with his *esh'g*. "You have me, *ya mashoogati*. How you do."

And he spent the rest of the night, pledged to spend the rest of his life, showing her just how.